WHAT COULD DISTRACT STEVIE FROM HORSES?

"Something's happened to Stevie," Lisa blurted out, trying to catch her breath. "We were on the phone and it suddenly went dead."

Concerned, Mrs. Lake and Lisa ran up the stairs to Stevie's bedroom. Without bothering to knock, they burst into the room.

"Stevie, are you—" Mrs. Lake stopped short.

Stevie was hovering over the incubator, her expression full of awe. One of the eggs was now definitely wiggling. Mrs. Lake and Lisa crept up beside Stevie, quietly taking a seat on the carpet beside the incubator to watch.

"It's hatching! It's hatching!"

Other books you will enjoy

CAMY BAKER'S HOW TO BE POPULAR
IN THE SIXTH GRADE by Camy Baker

HORSE CRAZY (The Saddle Club #1) by Bonnie Bryant

AMY, NUMBER SEVEN (Replica #1) by Marilyn Kaye

PURSUING AMY (Replica #2) by Marilyn Kaye

ANASTASIA ON HER OWN by Lois Lowry

THE BOYS START THE WAR/
THE GIRLS GET EVEN by Phyllis Reynolds Naylor

the SADDLE CLUB

HORSE FEATHERS

BONNIE BRYANT

A SKYLARK BOOK
NEW YORK • TORONTO • LONDON • SYDNEY • AUCKLAND

Special thanks to Sir "B" Farms and Laura Roper

RL 3.6, AGES 008–012

HORSE FEATHERS
A Bantam Skylark Book / May 2001

ISBN: 0-553-48740-X

Published simultaneously in the United States and Canada

Bantam Skylark is an imprint of Random House Children's Books. SKYLARK BOOK, BANTAM BOOKS, and the rooster colophon are registered trademarks of Random House, Inc. Bantam Books, 1540 Broadway, New York, New York 10036.

PRINTED IN THE UNITED STATES OF AMERICA

OPM 10 9 8 7 6 5 4 3 2 1

My special thanks to Sheila Prescott-Vessey for her help in the writing of this book.

I would also like to thank Jan Weber and Suzanne Detol of the American Vaulting Association for their gracious assistance and information on vaulting.

"MAX WAS VERY mysterious about the new schooling horse that's coming to the stable tomorrow," Lisa said excitedly.

"Did you see that smile on his face? He's definitely up to something," Stevie said.

It was a Saturday afternoon and Stevie Lake was walking home with her two best friends, Lisa Atwood and Carole Hanson. They'd just come from Pine Hollow Stables, where they'd had a Horse Wise meeting and a jumping lesson. Horse Wise was the name of Pine Hollow's Pony Club, run by Pine Hollow's owner, Max Regnery. Max also happened to be the Pony Club's director and the girls' riding instructor.

The girls hadn't been able to stop talking about Max's

surprise since he'd announced at the end of the jumping lesson that a new schooling horse was coming to Pine Hollow on Sunday, but just for a visit. There was obviously something very different and special about this horse, but whatever it was, Max was keeping it a secret.

"Maybe it's one of those Lipizzaner stallions from the Spanish Riding School in Vienna," speculated Stevie. "Or a jousting horse—like the kind they use in medieval festivals!" She paused for a moment to take a bite out of a carrot she'd saved from the bag of treats she'd brought for her horse, Belle. "What could be more special and different than that?" she asked.

Stevie had a habit of thinking big, which for most people would be a positive feature. But with Stevie it was more of a character flaw, since thinking big usually led to thinking bigger, and that often led to one of Stevie's crazy schemes. Her crazy schemes would often put her in hot water, and then Carole and Lisa would have to come to her rescue.

"Knowing Max, it's probably something that involves working hard and learning something new," Carole offered.

The girls nodded. Max was always making sure they learned new and interesting things about riding and horses.

Not that riding could ever become dull, thought Carole. If it were up to her, she'd be at the stables twenty-four hours a day, seven days a week, fifty-two weeks a year. She would choose to share a stall with her treasured gelding, Starlight, over a feather bed any day. Unfortunately, her father insisted that a proper education (one that involved time spent in the classroom, textbooks, and homework) took priority over horses. So Carole had to settle for being at Pine Hollow only a few hours a day, nearly seven days a week, nearly fifty-two weeks a year.

Pine Hollow Stables was a beautiful sprawling horse farm surrounded by acres of scenic pastures and miles of riding trails. The farm was located in Willow Creek, Virginia, outside of Washington, D.C., and housed over thirty horses and ponies, most of which were owned by Max and used for the school. Some of the students, like Stevie and Carole, boarded their own horses there. Lisa didn't have her own horse yet, but she regularly rode Prancer, an ex-racehorse that the girls had rescued.

Owning a horse required time and commitment. It also required money. In order to keep costs down and encourage teamwork, one of the requirements at Pine Hollow was that everyone who rode there had to help out with the barn chores. Well, almost everyone.

Veronica diAngelo, the barn prima donna, would never willingly participate in such distasteful tasks as mucking out stalls. Especially not when there were stable hands to do the work for her. Spoiled and used to having her way, Veronica was the worst example of a horseperson that the girls had ever met. More to the point, Veronica was the worst example of a *human being* that the girls had ever met. If there was an excuse not to pull her own weight, you could be sure that Veronica used it.

But Lisa, Stevie, and Carole didn't mind doing barn chores. They were more than willing to do anything that meant spending more time around the horses and the stable. The three girls knew almost from the moment they met that they shared a strong common bond: their love of horses. In fact, they were so horse-crazy, they had formed a group called The Saddle Club. There were only two rules for being a member: Number one, you had to be crazy about horses, and number two, all the members had to be willing to help each other out. To Stevie, Lisa, and Carole, those rules came as naturally and as effortlessly as breathing.

"I can't believe Max wouldn't even give us a hint about this mysterious horse," Lisa continued.

" 'Different and special,' " Stevie said, repeating

Max's words. "That could mean *anything*. Do you think I should have asked him for an itty bitty hint?"

Carole smiled. "You mean in addition to the first twenty times you asked him?"

"Well," Stevie said, grinning, "maybe all he needed was a little more encouragement."

Lisa shook her head doubtfully. "You know that no one keeps a secret better than Max."

"Hey, I keep a pretty good secret," Stevie replied innocently.

If there was anything that Stevie definitely *couldn't* keep, it was a secret. Worse yet, she could be so persistent that it made it hard for anyone around her to keep a secret, either.

"Maybe Red knows," Stevie suggested hopefully. "I'm sure if I cornered him, I could break him down eventually."

Carole and Lisa knew from experience that it was difficult, if not impossible, not to be swayed by Stevie's determination, or as some would call it, persistent pestering. And Red O'Malley was no exception. As the head stable hand at Pine Hollow, Red tended to know most of the goings-on there. But he was also extremely loyal to Max and enjoyed tormenting the students with anticipation almost as much as Max did. In this case, Carole suspected that Red knew all about Max's secret horse, and it was just as likely that he would never blow the surprise by telling them.

"This is torture," complained Stevie. "It's cruel and unusual punishment. How am I ever going to make it until tomorrow?"

"Well, the good news is that it's less than twenty-four hours away. Fifteen hours to be exact," Lisa calculated. "I guess you'll just have to wait and see."

"Wait and see?" repeated Stevie incredulously. Lisa, the most practical girl she knew, was always willing to offer practical (and on occasion annoyingly practical) advice. Anticipating Stevie's reaction, Lisa grinned mischievously and ducked behind Carole as Stevie playfully tried to punch her shoulder.

Carole rolled her eyes. "Lisa, did you forget who you were speaking to?"

Even Stevie laughed at that. *Wait and see* was not a phrase that Stevie liked to hear.

"Patience is a virtue, Stephanie Lake," Lisa teased further, mimicking Mrs. Lake's favorite expression when it came to her exuberant daughter.

"That's easy for you to say," Stevie grumbled good-naturedly. "You weren't born with this NTK gene that I've been afflicted with. I'm sure it's hereditary." *NTK* was Stevie's way of saying "need-to-know." And to be fair, her father suffered from the same gene, most noticeable when Stevie was the cause of a not-so-nice prank pulled on one of her brothers. Once, Stevie helped her twin brother, Alex, dye his hair orange for Halloween and purposely used a permanent dye. Another time Stevie's father picked her up at the stables and *needed* to know (quite emphatically) why her older brother Chad's underwear was on display at the neighborhood community center during a local hockey game. In Stevie's mind, surviving with an NTK gene was an unfortunate fact of life.

Not that Lisa *didn't* need to know things. In fact, she was a straight-A student and even did extra homework just so she could learn more. Stevie couldn't understand why someone would do homework instead of doing other stuff, fun stuff. And certainly no one but Lisa could ever consider homework fun. It was just that Lisa's need to know followed a more logical train of thought and wasn't likely to motivate her to, say, put salt in the sugar bowl just to see if anyone would notice, as Stevie had once done.

"Well, I just wish it were Sunday morning right now so that we wouldn't have to wait to meet the mystery horse," said Carole.

Carole was different from both Stevie and Lisa. If Stevie's need-to-know often sent her off on some crazy scheme, and Lisa's need-to-know got her straight As, then Carole's need-to-know applied only to horses. The only thing preventing Carole from achieving straight As in school was the subject matter. She could accurately list every breed of horse known in North America in alphabetical order, plus their significant—and not so significant—qualities, but she often had trouble recalling the names of the fifty states. She always made sure that the horses got watered and fed on time, but she sometimes forgot to eat breakfast or lunch herself.

Stevie and Lisa had long since realized that even though they were both horse-crazy, Carole was, hands down, the horse-craziest of all of them. Carole had no idea what she wanted to be when she grew up, but she knew for sure that it would involve horses. She had learned to ride almost before she could walk and was what Max liked to refer to as a natural rider. Lisa often thought that Carole galloping her gelding, Starlight, over a set of fences or through a large open field was the most graceful sight she'd ever seen. Stevie and Lisa knew that Carole was undoubtedly one of the best riders at Pine Hollow. Not that this went to Carole's head; Carole was appreciative and modest about her ability, constantly challenging herself to become even better.

"Hey, what's going on over there at your house?" asked Lisa.

Stevie squinted to see into the distance. From where they were, it looked like a small army had congregated on her front lawn. "Uh-oh."

"What did you do this time?" teased Carole. Being the only girl in a family of four children, Stevie was often the victim of practical jokes from her siblings. Unfortunately, Stevie was just as fond of instigating.

"Nothing that I know of," protested Stevie. She frowned, now able to make out her brothers, Chad, Michael, and Alex, gathered in the front yard. Her parents were there, too. That many of her family members in one location was never a good sign. Had she forgotten a family gathering? She quickly skimmed through her mental to-do list but couldn't come up with anything that accounted for the display.

She turned to Lisa. "Was I supposed to do something today?"

Lisa shook her head. "Not that I can remember."

"Maybe it's a surprise," suggested Carole.

Stevie shook her head. "If it were a surprise, they

wouldn't be standing on the front lawn where I can see them."

Carole nodded. "Well, intuition and past experience tell me that you're involved somehow."

Stevie straightened her shoulders, doing her best to appear offended. "Did it ever occur to you that I may not be the cause of this?" asked Stevie.

"Noooo!" chorused Lisa and Carole, which brought a smile to Stevie's face.

As the girls got closer, Stevie could see that her family appeared to be staring at something on the grass in the middle of their huddle. But from a distance Stevie couldn't make out what it was.

"What's the worst it could be?" Stevie asked, shrugging her shoulders.

Lisa and Carole exchanged looks.

"Okay, forget I asked that," said Stevie. "Come on, let's go find out."

The girls quickened their pace and cut across the street. They hurried up the driveway to the cluster of Lakes.

Stevie pushed into the small circle and peered over Michael's shoulder to get a look at the object of their attention. It was definitely not anything nearly as exciting as Stevie could have imagined. It was just a large wooden crate, with HANDLE WITH CARE stamped in big, bold red letters across the top of it.

Mr. Lake glanced up. "Ah, Stevie. I'm glad you're here. This was just delivered."

"What is it?" Stevie asked, now noticing the other suspicious words stamped on the crate, such as LIVESTOCK and OPEN IMMEDIATELY!

"We were hoping you could tell us," said Mrs. Lake.

"Me?" asked Stevie, surprised. "Why me?"

"Because it's addressed to you," said her older brother, Chad.

Stevie looked at Carole and Lisa, who had wiggled their way into the circle. Carole shrugged. Stevie, filled with uncertainty, took a cautious step toward the box. As she did, everyone else stepped back.

"It could be a bomb," said Michael. "They always hand deliver bombs on television."

Stevie shot Michael a look.

"Well it's true," he insisted.

"Don't be silly," said Mrs. Lake. "Whatever it is, it's not a bomb."

"Although the delivery man did warn us that it was very important to follow the instructions *exactly*," teased Mr. Lake.

"Stevie, don't pay any attention to them," said Mrs.

Lake, smiling her encouragement. But then, as if she couldn't help herself, she playfully took one small step backward, followed by Chad, Michael, Alex, and Mr. Lake. They seemed to be having an awful lot of fun at Stevie's expense.

"Very funny," said Stevie. She eyed the box warily. "I don't suppose anyone else wants to open it?" she asked hopefully.

"It's your box," Chad pointed out, his eyes twinkling mischievously as he took yet another step back.

"Maybe it's a present from Phil," suggested Lisa.

Phil Marsten was Stevie's boyfriend, and it wouldn't be unthinkable that he would send Stevie a present. Except that Stevie couldn't remember the last time Phil had ever had a present hand delivered, unless he was the one doing the delivering. And she certainly couldn't think of anything he'd give her that was this big.

"Here's a thought," Alex said impatiently. "Why don't you just open it and find out?"

Stevie took a closer look at the crate. It appeared to be heavily padded. She shrugged, "It's not like they would bother padding a bomb, right?"

Chad just grinned.

Stevie shook her head and took another step toward the box.

"Don't forget to follow the instructions," Mrs. Lake said.

"Follow the instructions," Stevie repeated, nodding.

Stevie decided to start with the most obvious instruction: HANDLE WITH CARE. She knelt beside the box and very carefully looked for a way to open it. There was a small latch on top, securing the lid. She slid it out of the way, then gently lifted the wooden panel. The inside of the box was lined with Styrofoam, which concealed its contents.

"What's in it?" Carole asked eagerly, leaning over Stevie's shoulder for a better view.

"I don't know. But there's some sort of battery pack keeping it warm." Stevie paused. "Isn't Styrofoam supposed to keep things cold?" Now she was really confused. What on earth could someone send her that required a temperature control?

"Is it ticking?" asked Michael.

Stevie put her ear closer. It *was* ticking. She jumped back. At least she *thought* she'd heard ticking.

"Boys, stop teasing your sister," admonished Mrs. Lake. "Go ahead, Stevie."

Encouraged, Stevie inspected the box closer and noticed a return address in small black type on one corner of the box. *If someone was going to send a bomb, they wouldn't give a return address*, Stevie reasoned. She glanced closer at the writing. It read: JOB'S COMFORTERS, followed by a mailing address.

"Job's Comforters!" squealed Stevie excitedly, immediately forgetting her apprehension about the crate. "Maybe it's the down quilt I've been hoping for!"

"Stevie, if it were a quilt, why would they need to keep it warm?" Lisa pointed out.

Stevie frowned. "They wouldn't. Unless of course they wanted to make sure it was nice and toasty when I received it," she tried hopefully.

But her whole family, as well as Lisa and Carole, shook their heads in response. Whatever it was, it was definitely not a down quilt.

Stevie carefully and somewhat nervously plucked off another layer of Styrofoam. There, beneath the Styrofoam, was a compact heating box. She searched her mind for things in the store that might have come with a heating unit. But she came up blank. Even more curiously, the top of the heating box was dotted with small holes.

Stevie peered closely at the top of the box. "Could it be . . ." She paused midsentence as a thought occurred to her. She looked again at the writing on the outside of the box.

"Livestock?" whispered Stevie. She very cautiously

put her eye to one of the holes and peered inside the heating box. "Uh-oh . . ."

"Well, what is it?" Alex demanded impatiently. "Move over so I can look."

Stevie rocked back on one foot, allowing Alex to have a peek. "Is that what I think it is?" she asked uncertainly.

Alex stared through the hole for a long moment. Then he glanced over at Stevie, his face showing the same expression that hers had moments before. "Uh-oh . . ."

Stevie sighed. "That's what I thought." She quickly took another glance through the small holes in the top of the box, just to be sure. But nothing had changed. There, in front of her eyes, or in front of one eye to be more exact, were twelve large eggs, gently nestled in an incubator.

"Stevie! Tell us what it is!" Lisa said impatiently.

"Eggs," said Stevie flatly.

"Eggs?" echoed Carole and Lisa as if they'd misheard her.

Everyone stared at Stevie, their faces full of confusion, waiting for further explanation.

Stevie shrugged helplessly and glanced down at the box. "I think I'm going to be a mom."

2

NEEDLESS TO SAY, dinner at the Lake house that night was louder than normal, with the eggs being the obvious choice of conversation. Stevie had even convinced her parents to allow her to bring the crate into the dining room where she could keep an eye on it during dinner. She'd already left the table three times to peek through the holes.

On Stevie's fourth trip to the crate, Mrs. Lake finally said, "Dear, they're not going to hatch while we're eating. Finish your dinner and then you can spend as much time as you like with them."

Stevie grudgingly made her way back to the table,

sitting slightly turned in her chair to keep one eye on the crate.

"Stevie," prompted Carole excitedly, "tell us what the letter said." She was referring to the crisp white envelope resting on the table beside Stevie's elbow.

On closer inspection of the crate, Alex had found the letter slipped between the incubator and the battery pack. It was addressed to Ms. Stephanie Lake, which obviously meant that the eggs had been delivered to the correct house and that it was not a grocery delivery mix-up as Michael had suggested when they'd carried the crate into the house.

"Well," Stevie said casually, "remember the other week, Mom, when we went to the Bed 'n' Bath Shop?" Mrs. Lake nodded. "And I had to wait while you searched the *entire* store for a purple bath pillow that was the *exact* same color as the purple flowers in the wallpaper in the upstairs bathroom?" Mrs. Lake nodded patiently. "And it took *forever*?"

"Your point, Stevie?" said Mrs. Lake, smiling at her daughter's flare for the dramatic.

"Well, I was standing there, aging by the minute"—Stevie continued, ignoring her mother, who rolled her eyes—"and I noticed this contest being hosted by Job's Comforters. First prize was a down comforter."

"But Stevie, you have a comforter already," said Mr. Lake, clearly not grasping the significance of down versus synthetic fiber.

"Dad," replied Stevie patiently, "a down comforter isn't just like any comforter. It's filled with *down*. Trust me, there's a huge difference."

Mr. Lake nodded slowly, knowing that when in doubt, the best defense was to nod.

Stevie continued, "Now, let me also remind everyone that a down comforter *was* at the top of my wish list *last* Christmas. Which, in case no one has noticed, has come and gone."

"You mean, at the top of your list right under the four million horse-related items," joked Chad.

"The point is I didn't get one. So, I thought, maybe, just maybe, I'd win one."

"You won the contest?" Mr. Lake asked, getting confused.

Stevie hesitated. "Well, if you can call it that. I won sixth prize. Not the comforter, not the down jacket—which, let me add, would have been the most practical choice to keep me toasty warm at the barn this winter—not the comforter cover, third place; not the pillow, fourth place; not even the mittens, fifth place—which, let me point out, also would have been a bonus for those long winter horseback rides along the snow-covered trails to keep my fingers toasty warm. But nooooo. Instead I won sixth place: a dozen goose eggs and an incubator."

"Let me guess," said Mr. Lake lightly. "Practical only if you're short on breakfast items for the weekend."

Chad almost choked on his carrots and Mrs. Lake covered her mouth with her napkin to try to disguise her smile. Stevie ignored them all.

"I guess, when you think about it," she mused, "there *is* a connection between the eggs and the comforter. It's sort of like a make-your-own comforter." She glanced over at the eggs, which had yet to hatch, and therefore had yet to produce down. "It'll just be a little more time-consuming."

"Not to mention slightly traumatizing for your little friends over there," said Chad, indicating the crate.

Stevie frowned, confused.

Chad explained. "Well, the only way to get down off of a goose, Stevie, is severely and permanently unpleasant for the animal, although it may add something special to our Saturday-night dinners." He grinned, displaying an even row of white teeth.

Stevie's eyes darted protectively toward the crate.

She suddenly had terrifying visions of those twelve little yet-to-be-born eggs becoming someone's comforter stuffing. It just wasn't possible!

"We can't let that happen," Stevie finally croaked. "Mom, Dad"—She glanced around the table desperately— "these particular eggs are definitely *not* comforter material." She looked to Carole and Lisa for support. "I mean, have you ever seen eggs that looked more *un*like comforter material than those?"

"Absolutely not comforter eggs," agreed Carole.

"Too . . . eggy," added Lisa. Stevie gave her an odd look, and Lisa shrugged helplessly.

"See!" exclaimed Stevie. "We need to help these eggs keep their down! I mean, these future goslings."

Mrs. Lake, who already had a pretty good idea of where this conversation was headed, said gently, "Stevie, you know we can't possibly keep them."

"Mom! If we don't, they could end up as part of someone's decor!" Stevie turned pleading eyes toward her father. "Dad, please, I promise I'll take care of them. I'll feed them, I'll clean up after them, and I'll love them with all my heart. I swear. Double swear," she said earnestly. "Please, Dad, pleeease."

"Stevie," her father began skeptically, "we need to

be practical about this. For one thing, geese are outdoor birds. They don't belong in a house."

"Well, I wouldn't say they don't belong, exactly," quipped Chad, tapping his dinner plate teasingly. "Served up with mashed potatoes and gravy, I think they'd be quite acceptable."

Stevie noticed Lisa quickly and discreetly tucking her napkin into the top of her T-shirt, spreading it out to cover as much space as possible. Carole was doing the same thing. Stevie knew the two girls had had enough dinners at the Lake house to know an invitation to a food fight when they heard one. And Stevie, who was extremely efficient with a spoon and a bowl of food, needed very little in the way of motivation when it came to getting even with her brothers.

"Stevie!" Mr. Lake's warning shout halted Stevie just as she reached for the bowl of mashed potatoes, clearly intending to catapult a wad in Chad's direction. Mr. Lake put out his hand. "I'll take that."

Grudgingly, Stevie handed over the bowl, having to satisfy herself with an evil glare at Chad.

"Well, I think it'd be cool," said Michael. "I've never had a pet goose before. It could sleep in my bed and share my pillow and everything."

"There," declared Stevie. "Finally someone with an appropriate appreciation for waterfowl."

"You know how you like to play by the pond in town?" Alex asked Michael.

Michael nodded.

"And you know those little mementos that the geese leave that you always end up slipping in and they end up all over your shoes?" Alex continued.

Michael nodded again.

"Well, I hate to break it to you, but they go where the geese go."

Michael's mouth formed a small o as he thought about that. "Ewww . . ." He turned to Stevie. "Changed my mind."

Stevie rolled her eyes in frustration. "Look, if it helps, I'll litter train them. How hard can it be?" She looked again to her parents. "Please, please, please?"

Mr. and Mrs. Lake exchanged glances as Stevie held her breath. Then her mother nodded. "You can keep the goslings—"

Mrs. Lake's announcement was momentarily interrupted by Stevie's squeal of joy.

"—as long as you agree to be solely responsible for them," Mrs. Lake finished. "But first they have to hatch!"

"I absolutely promise," Stevie chattered excitedly as she jumped up from the table to hug her parents.

"I guess you'd better start practicing your goose skills," teased Chad. He stuck his fists under his armpits, flapped his "wings," and said, "Quack quack!"

"Mother Goose!" squealed Michael. "Stevie's going to be Mother Goose!"

Stevie, still too excited from her mother's announcement, wasn't even bothered by her brothers' teasing. In fact, she thought *Mother Goose* kind of had a nice ring to it.

Suddenly, a loud, distinctly catlike howl added to the commotion. It was a sound of pure glee.

"Madonna!" Stevie shouted.

In total panic, Stevie raced back around the table to find her cat poised on the crate, trying to squeeze one calico paw through the small openings in the top of the box. "Madonna, no!" she scolded. She quickly scooped up the delinquent feline and walked into the living room, dropping her gently on the couch. "There will be no more of that," she told the cat firmly.

Madonna, offended at being expelled from the dining room, pulled herself up to her full regal height of nine inches. With great dignity, she jumped up onto the back of the sofa to stare out the window, turning her back to Stevie.

As Madonna began cleaning her paws, Stevie glanced back nervously at the crate. She was beginning to get the feeling that being Mother Goose would be harder than she thought. And the eggs weren't even hatched yet.

"Stevie," Mrs. Lake suggested, "why don't you take the eggs up to your room where they'll be less of a temptation?" Then she added, "For everyone," as she glared at her sons.

Stevie glanced back at Madonna, still perched on top of the sofa. The cat had turned around and her eyes were now fixed on the crate as her tail twitched in anticipation.

"Good idea," Stevie said quickly.

Carole and Lisa immediately excused themselves from the dinner table to help Stevie carry the crate upstairs. The girls gently placed the crate on the floor of Stevie's bedroom, and Stevie shut her door behind them.

"As long as we keep the door closed, the eggs should be safe from any further Madonna trauma," said Stevie, walking back to the crate. She knelt in front of the box. Carole took a seat beside her. Lisa sat at Stevie's desk, reaching for the instructions that had come with the eggs.

"Okay," said Lisa, opening the folded instructions, "let's see how to take care of your eggs."

While Lisa skimmed through the material, Stevie and Carole gently pulled the incubator and battery pack out of the crate, placing it on the floor beside them.

"It says here that you'll need to keep the eggs at a constant temperature until they hatch," read Lisa.

"That explains the thermostat in the incubator," said Stevie, peering through the glass top of the incubator. Then she checked the sticker on the side of the box for the correct temperature, which varied depending on how old the eggs were. The thermostat read 99.5 degrees, which was the correct temperature for eggs incubated under twenty-five days. And according to the date on the label, the eggs were on day twenty-three.

"Oh, and very importantly, you need to turn the eggs every four hours until they hatch so that they don't spend too long on any one side."

"Every *four* hours?" Carole repeated, shocked. "Stevie, that's impossible."

"No it isn't," Stevie answered confidently. "I'll turn them before I go to school in the morning, then again when I come home for lunch—"

"You don't come home for lunch," said Lisa.

"Well, I do now. I'll turn them again at dinner, and

then I'll set my alarm to make sure I don't miss any of the night turnings."

"You're going to get up in the middle of the night?" Carole sounded skeptical.

"Piece of cake." Stevie waved off the words with a toss of her hand.

"Well, then we'd better get to bed," said Lisa, "since you have to get up in four hours."

The girls pulled their pajamas out of their backpacks and quickly got changed. This was a traditional part of the sleepover—to snuggle under the bedcovers or into their sleeping bags and talk about horses until they could no longer keep their eyes open. Only this time, Stevie's thoughts remained on her incubated eggs.

"I'm going to dream that it's tomorrow and the mystery horse has just arrived," said Carole as she snuggled into her sleeping bag.

Lisa smiled, yawning sleepily. "While you're at it, maybe you can ask Max what this horse does that's so different and special. And if he tells you, wake me up and let me know so that I don't have to wait until tomorrow."

"I wonder what color they'll be," said Stevie, crawling into bed.

"Liver chestnut with four white stockings and a blaze." Carole sighed dreamily.

Stevie shook her head absentmindedly. "I don't think they come in chestnut. They could just be white. Or maybe brown-and-black with the colorful tail feathers. It said in the letter that there could be as many as four different breeds of geese in the bunch."

Carole and Lisa exchanged concerned looks. It wasn't like Stevie to confuse equines with waterfowl. Especially on a Saturday and especially during their bedtime horse talk. "Stevie, I was talking about the mystery horse. You know, Max's surprise for tomorrow? Ten whole hours away, which earlier was making you crazy?"

"Oh, I can't believe I nearly forgot!" exclaimed Stevie.

"That's better," teased Lisa.

Then Lisa and Carole watched with confused expressions as Stevie jumped out of bed and grabbed a pencil off the desk. "I have to mark the eggs."

Carole and Lisa sat up to watch as Stevie gently took each egg out of the incubator and put a thin pencil line down one side before replacing it. That way, when she turned the eggs, she explained, she would be able to turn them evenly.

"So, I understand that Veronica will be riding Belle in our next jumping lesson," Lisa said casually as Stevie reached for egg number six.

"Huh?" Stevie said distractedly. Then, without waiting for Lisa's response, she replied, "Oh, that's nice."

Carole and Lisa exchanged surprised looks. Typically the mere mention of Veronica's name was enough to send Stevie into a slow burn, but the idea of Stevie's worst enemy riding her beloved mare, Belle, should have caused an explosion beyond measure. Instead, Stevie was still calmly drawing lines on her eggs. This was serious.

"There," said Stevie as she replaced the last egg in the incubator. She crawled back into bed and reached for her alarm clock. She set the alarm for the next turning. It hardly seemed worth going to sleep. On the other hand, she *was* pretty tired. Stevie took one last look at the eggs lying peacefully in the incubator, then lay back in the bed, fluffing a pillow under her head. "You know," she said, staring up at the ceiling, "this could be a great opportunity to learn something new."

"I'm sure that's exactly what Max has in mind," said Lisa.

"And when it come to horses," Carole added happily, "I'm always up to learning something new."

Stevie stared at her friends, wondering how they could possibly get so off the topic so quickly. "I was talking about the eggs," she said slowly. "You know, the ones we've been talking about all evening?"

Lisa looked over at Stevie—checking to make sure that it really was Stevie. It certainly looked like Stevie. And it even sounded like Stevie, except for the non-horse-related words that kept coming out of her mouth. "Goodnight, Stevie," said Lisa.

Carole burrowed further into her sleeping bag. *Not to worry*, she thought. *Stevie will be back to her old self the moment her head hits the pillow.* She took a quick peek at Stevie and realized that her head was already on the pillow. *Okay, first thing in the morning*, Carole corrected herself.

It wasn't that Stevie didn't get obsessed about things—it would be un-Stevie-like *not* to get obsessed. But one thing that Carole knew for sure was that nothing—*nothing*—distracted Stevie for long from thinking about horses. Certainly not a bunch of eggs in a box. And certainly not when there was a mystery horse arriving at Pine Hollow in less than ten hours.

Stevie clicked off the lamp beside her bed, leaving the room in darkness except for the light shining in the incubator. There was a moment of silence, followed by Stevie's anxious question: "Do you think there's any chance they might hatch early?"

Lisa pulled her sleeping bag over her head and gave a muffled "Brrumpf!" in response.

3

THE ALARM WENT off at exactly 6:00 the next morning. Carole's hand slipped out from under her sleeping bag to shut it off. *Four hours since the last time it went off*, Carole thought groggily, although it felt more like only four minutes. She rolled onto her side to go back to sleep when she suddenly remembered what day it was—Sunday! Max's mystery horse was arriving that morning! Carole bolted upright, intending to wake Lisa and Stevie, only to find that Stevie's bed was already empty.

"Tell me it's not morning already," Lisa mumbled.

Stevie was sitting cross-legged on the floor by the incubator, staring at the eggs. She glanced over. "It's about time you two sleepyheads woke up."

Lisa peeked out from her sleeping bag at the sound of Stevie's perky voice. Stevie was usually the last of the girls to wake up. "Who are you and what have you done with the real Stevie Lake?" Lisa asked.

Carole rubbed her eyes to make sure she was really seeing what she was seeing. "Stevie, what are you doing?"

Stevie grinned. "Watching."

"Why? Have they changed shape?" Lisa teased as she sat up and stretched.

"I thought they weren't supposed to hatch for nearly another week," said Carole.

"Well, what if they decide to come early and I'm not watching?" Stevie asked in a logical tone that almost sounded like Lisa—except that it was Stevie and it wasn't logical at all that she should sound like Lisa. "The instructions said I could expect some hatching within the next week, so I'll just sit here until it does."

Lisa sighed and climbed out of her sleeping bag. Now *that* sounded like the Stevie she knew and loved. She padded across the soft carpet to peek at the eggs. They definitely didn't look like they were going to hatch anytime soon. "I think you can relax for a few days, Stevie."

"Besides," said Carole as she tried to run a brush through

her tangled curls, "have you forgotten that Max's new mystery horse is arriving today? We can't miss that!"

Stevie hesitated, torn between curiosity about the new schooling horse and leaving her little charges alone for a few hours.

"They'll be fine," said Lisa, reading Stevie's thoughts.

"Plus, if Max *has* gotten one of those magnificent jousting horses and you aren't there to see it . . ." sighed Carole.

That did it. "I guess I could leave them for a little while," Stevie replied quickly. She checked the thermostat. It still read 99.5 degrees, as it had the last five times she'd checked it that morning.

Stevie affectionately patted the top of the incubator. "I'll just be gone a little while," she whispered to the eggs. "Don't do anything I wouldn't do." She caught Lisa's and Carole's questioning looks. "On second thought, don't do anything at all. Just sit there and be . . . eggy."

The girls got dressed in their riding clothes and went downstairs to eat breakfast. An hour later they were out the door.

THE SADDLE CLUB arrived at Pine Hollow Stables just in time to see a large horse trailer being pulled up the long drive ahead of them. They could barely contain their excitement and broke into a run, reaching the truck just as the driver was releasing the bolt on the rear door of the trailer. Max and Red were already there, waiting to unload the new arrival.

"Good morning, girls," said Max. "I was starting to think you weren't going to make it in time to see Clara arrive."

"Are you kidding?" said Carole. "I barely slept a wink last night!"

"Neither did I," Lisa grumbled good-naturedly, "but I think it had more to do with Stevie's alarm clock going off every four hours than it did the mystery horse."

Max frowned curiously and seemed ready to ask Lisa what she meant by that when the back door of the trailer opened. The driver slowly backed a large, rather unpromising-looking horse down the ramp. All the girls could see at first was a wide black-and-white rump.

Red and Max moved in to help with the unloading. A few moments later the large horse stood on the driveway in front of them, sniffing gently at Max's front pocket for a treat. Max handed the lead line over to Red, then followed the driver to his truck to sign the release papers.

"I don't think it's a jousting horse," Stevie said slowly. "Or if it is, it isn't what I imagined."

"It looks like a workhorse," Carole said, her brow

wrinkling slightly. "I wonder what Max thinks we could learn from this horse. It doesn't even appear to be a riding horse!"

"I got up early for this?" Veronica snorted disdainfully. The Saddle Club turned to see Veronica standing behind them, completely unimpressed. "It's just an old nag—hardly a decent piece of horseflesh."

"Just because it's not a Thoroughbred doesn't mean it's not a decent horse," retorted Stevie, furious at Veronica's rude remarks.

Stevie could already see that the mare had a kind and inquisitive look in her eye as she glanced at her new surroundings. The longer Stevie stared at the horse, the more impressed she was. The mare was large and heavyset, but she walked beside Red with an easy grace, matching his stride, even though his was probably much shorter than her own. As Red approached the girls the mare whinnied a greeting to Starlight, who had run up to the paddock fence. Starlight whinnied back.

"Looks like she's already made a new friend," observed Lisa.

Stevie and Carole smiled.

Max finished signing the papers, then hurried over to take the lead line from Red. He was positively beaming. "Girls, I would like you to meet Clara." Without waiting for a response, he led the large mare across the driveway toward the barn. "Come on, let's give her a proper Pine Hollow welcome," he called out over his shoulder.

"Well, I personally have better things to do than brush down a lawn ornament," said Veronica. She spun on her heel and made her way toward the grass paddocks, where Danny, her sleek dapple-gray Thoroughbred, awaited her.

As Max and Red disappeared inside the barn with Clara, the girls exchanged confused looks.

"I hate to say this," Lisa started slowly, "but Veronica almost has a point."

"That big old mare is hardly what Max needs for young riders. She's so wide, they'd barely be able to fit on her, much less ride her," said Carole.

"Maybe the pressures of running the stable have finally gone to Max's head and he's flipped out," suggested Stevie. It was the only thing that made sense. "Students would be better off walking on Clara than riding her."

Carole's face suddenly broke into a grin. "That's it, of course!" she exclaimed excitedly. "That's Max's surprise!"

Stevie and Lisa exchanged bewildered looks—perhaps Carole had gone over the edge along with Max. "Do you think I should order two straitjackets instead of just one?" Stevie asked Lisa.

"Don't you get it? That's exactly what this horse has been trained for. To be walked on, stood on, jumped on, and cartwheeled over," Carole told them eagerly. "We're going to do some vaulting!"

"Vaulting?" Lisa said curiously.

Carole turned toward the barn. Stevie and Lisa followed.

"Well, I've never actually done it," began Carole, "but I've read about it. It's like gymnastics on horseback. And actually, it goes back to the times of the early Romans, who used vaulting techniques to jump over charging bulls. And during the Middle Ages, the knights did various forms of vaulting in order to increase their agility and balance on horseback while in armor. They also invented different vaulting moves to quickly mount and dismount their horses in battle."

"That's very good, Carole," Max said as the girls walked down the aisle to where Clara was settling into her new stall. "In fact, in Germany new riders are often required to do a year of vaulting before moving on to other forms of riding, such as dressage or jumping."

"Wouldn't it be easier to learn how to ride, and *then* learn how to perform gymnastics on a moving horse?" questioned Lisa. She remembered her first experience on horseback—the simple act of sitting on a horse in motion, which Carole and Stevie had made look easy, had been difficult enough. She couldn't imagine trying to add gymnastics to the mix. As a beginner she thought she'd spent more time in the dirt than in the saddle!

As the girls helped Max settle Clara into her new surroundings, bringing her fresh hay and water, Max confirmed their suspicion that Clara was going to teach them vaulting and answered Lisa's question.

"Vaulting is a wonderful training foundation for every other kind of riding because balance is such a critical issue for every rider. When done correctly, it not only inspires confidence, but also teaches you to understand and gain a feel for the natural motion of the horse."

"I can't wait to try it," said Carole.

Lisa and Stevie nodded in agreement. Stevie had to admit that a vaulting horse was starting to sound almost as exciting as a jousting horse.

Max smiled. "Well, why don't you girls give Clara a quick grooming, then we'll start with our first vaulting lesson."

As Max left to ready the arena for their lesson, the girls entered Clara's stall, equipped with brushes, currycombs, and a hoof pick.

Lisa laughed as Clara very softly nuzzled her hair. "There, now, girl," she said, stroking Clara's velvety nose. For such a big horse, she was incredibly gentle.

Carole moved to Clara's far side and stood next to

her high wither, which was well out of Carole's short reach. "I'd better get a stool," she said.

As Carole left the stall, Stevie pointed toward Clara's hooves. "Remind me not to get stomped by one of those," she chuckled.

Lisa poked her head around Clara's wide shoulder and looked down. "I can't believe I didn't notice Clara's hooves before—they're the size of dinner plates! How am I going to pick them up to clean them?" she asked incredulously. But to her surprise, when she leaned against Clara's shoulder to ask her to raise her foot, the mare did so willingly. Lisa cupped the large front hoof in one hand, resting the weight of it on her knee, and began picking out the frog to make sure no stones had gotten wedged into the sole on the trip over.

Once the girls got accustomed to Clara's size, they realized she was just like any other horse in the barn. Her gentle manner soon won the girls over completely. They finished grooming her, and, with a gentle pat on her big black nose and a couple of treats, they ran off to report to Max for their first vaulting lesson.

4

"I THINK MY legs are going to fall off," protested Lisa, trying to keep her balance on Prancer while she sat in the saddle and pedaled her legs in the air while holding her arms out at shoulder level.

"I don't understand the point of having a perfectly good vaulting horse in the barn if we're going to spend the whole lesson riding our own horses," added Stevie. It wasn't that she was complaining exactly. She loved riding Belle. It was just that their lesson was nearly over and the girls hadn't seen hide nor hair of Clara.

"I'm actually having fun," Carole said brightly, concentrating on executing the same pedaling movements as Lisa and Stevie, only somehow managing to do them better.

Stevie shook her head in amazement. Carole was the only person she knew who could have fun doing torturous balancing exercises on horseback.

"Good boy," Carole murmured to Starlight as he maintained an even walk around the edge of the arena.

"Let's see those knees nice and high," shouted Max from the middle of the arena, turning to keep his eye on each student as they passed.

"I mean, why would he bring her here if he's not going to let us ride her?" whispered Lisa, struggling to lift her aching legs higher in the pedaling motion.

"This is ridiculous," snorted Veronica. Like most of the students, she was having trouble maintaining her balance. The pedaling motion caused her to tip forward, which Danny mistook for a cue to trot. Veronica's hands instinctively flew to the reins, jerking the muscular gray Thoroughbred back to a walk.

"Veronica," scolded Max. "You know better than to pull on his mouth like that. Danny's increased speed was a direct response to your body position. Balance is the key to all forms of riding," he reminded the students. "An unbalanced rider begets an unbalanced horse."

"Not to mention the increased likelihood of a face-plant in the dirt," joked Stevie.

Max smiled. "Not exactly the way I would have described it, but yes. Okay, that's enough pedaling."

There was a chorus of relieved sighs as the students lowered their legs and replaced their feet in the stirrups.

"For our next exercise," explained Max, "we're going to perform an around-the-world in the saddle. Everyone tie up your reins."

Carole smiled, knotting her reins behind Starlight's neck so that they wouldn't slip down and possibly trip him when she released them. The around-the-world was one of her favorite exercises. It meant that the riders, without the use of their arms, had to execute a 360-degree turn while the horse was in motion, pausing halfway around to ride backward for five strides.

On Max's command, Carole dutifully pulled her feet from the stirrups, holding out her arms for balance. She carefully swung her right leg over Starlight's withers, bringing it to a rest against his left side. Then she swung her left leg over his rump, sitting backward in the saddle. "Steady boy," Carole whispered softly to Starlight. Familiar with the exercise, Starlight nickered in response and maintained an even forward gait, even though Carole was no longer holding the reins.

Belle followed behind Starlight, watching Carole curiously. Carole giggled to herself, thinking that the whole class looked a little silly sitting backward while their horses continued to walk steadily around the ring.

"Very good, everyone," Max said as they completed the exercise. "Hang in there, we're almost done. For the next exercise, I want you to touch your ankles together, front and back. No cheating," Max teased, eliciting a synchronized groan from the class. He smiled at the response.

"Well, as I for one have no intention of standing on a horse, these exercises are a waste of my time," grumbled Veronica, who had been doing the exercises with minimal effort.

"As a reward," continued Max, "whoever does it first is excused from the rest of the class."

With a sudden about-face, Veronica gracefully swung her feet to the back above Danny's rump, held the position for five seconds, and then swung them to the front above his withers, finishing the exercise while most of the class was still struggling to hold the first position.

"Very good, Veronica," Max congratulated her. "You're excused. Take Danny for a walk to cool him out."

Veronica quickly hopped off Danny and loosened

his girth. She glanced over her shoulder and smirked at The Saddle Club. "Enjoy the rest of the class."

Stevie turned to Carole. "Have I ever mentioned that she annoys me?"

"This week, today, or in the last hour?" Carole responded sardonically.

Stevie grinned. "Well, I for one *do* intend to stand on a horse," she declared, perfectly imitating Veronica's snobby tone. "And I also intend to do these exercises, even if they kill me."

"I agree," said Carole. "Max wouldn't be giving us these exercises unless they were important."

Lisa nodded her agreement.

With renewed energy, the girls threw themselves into all the exercises Max gave them and even surprised him by asking for more.

"Okay, that's enough for today," Max said finally. "Put away your horses. And once you're done, meet me outside in the grass ring for part two of the vaulting exercises."

"Part two?" Lisa groaned. "I think I just used up all my energy in part one."

"That's where our second wind comes in," joked Stevie. "At least I hope it does."

The girls quickly untacked and groomed their

horses, making sure that they each had fresh water and plenty of hay before hurrying out to find Max.

They were surprised to find that the grass ring had been transformed into an exercise area. Blue foam-padded gym mats were strewn about the ring. To one side of the mats was a four-inch-high balance beam. But even more surprising to the girls was the oil drum in the center of the ring. A set of handles were attached to the top of the barrel, and the barrel itself was padded with several layers of carpet and covered with heavy denim cloth.

"Everyone gather around," Max called out.

The last of the riders appeared, including a not-so-enthusiastic Veronica, and circled around Max.

"I'm sure you're all wondering what that's for," said Max, pointing to the barrel. "Anyone want to take a guess?"

"We're going to practice bull riding?" Stevie offered humorously.

The class laughed in response.

Carole put up her hand. Max nodded and pointed to her.

"It looks like a practice vaulting barrel," said Carole. "I've read that they're used by the vaulters to learn the moves before they get on the horse. It's safer for both the rider and the mount."

Max nodded. "Very good, Carole. You're exactly right."

Then he explained to the class, "Both the balance beam and the practice barrel are very important to help you establish balance. You need to learn how to do the exercises on a static object before trying it on a moving animal. The most familiar saying in vaulting is that if you can't do it on the ground or on the barrel, then you're not going to do it on *my* horse."

Everyone laughed at the joke, although they realized Max had a good point.

"Let's get started!" Max shouted.

As the last student finished the beam exercises, Max called the class over to the vaulting barrel. "One of the first things we'll need to learn before we get *on* the horse is how to get *off* the horse safely, in case of an emergency."

Although most of the riders were familiar with the exercise, Max walked the class through the emergency dismount just to be sure. The most important thing was to jump clear of the horse's hooves and to roll with the momentum of the dismount, to prevent any type of impact injury. For practice, Max had the class try several emergency dismounts by leaping from the barrel to the ground.

Once he was satisfied that everyone was dismounting correctly, he surprised the class by calling Red in to demonstrate a couple of the more common vaulting positions on the barrel. Red gracefully performed several different moves, including one called the Mill, in which the vaulter made a complete rotation on the barrel in four evenly counted phases, carrying each leg over the barrel in a high semicircle.

"That explains why Max had us do the around-the-world earlier," said Stevie. "What it doesn't explain is how he"—Stevie pointed to Red—"managed to make that look so easy."

Red overheard the comment and laughed, then exchanged looks with Max.

Max smiled. "We cheated a little. Red spent a few years on a vaulting team before he moved to Willow Creek, which is why I thought he'd be the best person to act as our longeur." Max's voice went serious, as it always did when he was trying to get across an important point about riding. "Our number one concern is safety, for you and for Clara. Only a person with the experience to keep the horse moving forward at a safe and steady pace should be handling the longe line."

As if anticipating the next question, Red said, "I know that you all know how to longe a horse. But it's one thing to send a horse forward as a form of exercise. It's quite another to control its every step."

"And here I thought longeing was the easy part," said Carole. Everyone laughed.

Max signaled for a ten-minute break, and the girls ran inside the barn for a quick drink.

"I hope we can all watch the eggs hatch together," Stevie said as she reached into her cubby for her water bottle. She suddenly realized that it was the first time she had thought about the eggs all day. "Oh my gosh! What time is it?" she exclaimed, grabbing Lisa's hand to check her watch. It was just after two o'clock. She had missed the midday turning of the eggs. "My eggs!"

Stevie shot off at full speed down the barn aisle, passing Veronica, who was taking a sip of her soda.

"What's with her?" Veronica asked in a bored manner.

Lisa and Carole exchanged looks, then said in unison, as if no further explanation was necessary: "Mother Goose."

STEVIE RACED UP the stairs and burst into her bedroom, dreading the result of her missed turning. She'd only had the eggs for a day and already she was neglecting them. Some Mother Goose she was!

Stevie knelt beside the incubator, opened the lid, and very gently turned each egg. Then she grabbed the instructions. She sat back on her heels and went through them, line by line, to see if she might have done any permanent damage to the eggs.

From what she read it seemed as if the eggs would be all right. Not that it prevented her from being nervous. She checked and rechecked the temperature and humidity—everything was normal. Still, she was reluctant to leave, even though it meant missing the rest of her lesson.

What if she had actually done damage and she just couldn't tell yet? And then what if she left and the damage got worse? *The safest thing is just to stay with them,* she thought. With that decision made, she crawled onto her desk chair and leaned against the back of it, never once taking her eyes off the incubator.

Stevie was still sitting in the same position, staring at the incubator, when Lisa and Carole knocked on her bedroom door two hours later.

"Tell me you haven't been sitting there this whole time," said Carole, concerned.

Stevie looked at her guiltily. "Failure to turn," she said seriously, "and it's only the second day. How bad is that?"

Lisa came over and gently patted Stevie's shoulder. "Stevie, the instructions allow a caretaker a good night's sleep. And I read that the eggs are fine as long as you keep alternating the side that's up, night after night. I really don't think a few extra hours will have affected them."

"Besides," added Carole, "the eggs are in their last week of incubation and should be almost to the point where they don't need to be turned at all."

"Maybe so, but I'm not taking any more chances,"

Stevie announced determinedly. "They're not leaving my sight until they hatch."

"Have you forgotten about school?" Lisa asked gently.

"Oh, right. Well, I'll just come home for lunch every day to turn them." Then she suddenly remembered that they hadn't told her about the last part of the vaulting lesson. "Oh! What did I miss?"

"Only the part where we actually got a chance to longe Clara," Lisa said casually.

"And the part where Max explained to us about the different types of vaulting teams," added Carole.

"Oh sure, he exercises us to death, and then the second I leave all the exciting stuff happens," Stevie said with a frown.

Carole smiled and eagerly filled Stevie in on the types of vaulting teams that were allowed in competition. The first one was made up of eight riders and a longeur; the second was an individual rider and a longeur; and the third was commonly referred to as a *pas de deux*, which Max had explained was technically a young woman, a young man, and a longeur. However, if two vaulters of the same sex participated, it was called pairs. In every case, though, the longeur was a very important part of the team because he or she had to be able to keep the horse going at a steady pace.

"Of course, the type of teams are only important if we're actually going to compete," Lisa told Stevie. "Unfortunately, Max said that we only have Clara for a month—not exactly enough time to prepare for a real competition."

"But," Carole broke in excitedly, "on Clara's last weekend at Pine Hollow, Max is going to let us demonstrate what we've learned in our own mini-competition."

"Which doesn't give us very much time to prepare," said Lisa.

"And Mrs. Welch, Clara's owner, has offered to be the judge," Carole added. "Isn't that cool?"

Stevie was still stuck on the one-month part. After the trouble she'd had with some of the exercises earlier that day, she couldn't imagine that a month would be enough time to learn how to vault.

Lisa continued. "Max actually said that it's not as hard as it looks." Then she corrected herself. "Or, that it is, but if we work hard, we should all be vaulting by the end of the month—"

Lisa was interrupted by a knock on the door. Or more accurately, there was a quick perfunctory knock one second before all three of Stevie's brothers tromped into the room. Stevie jumped to her feet, trying to push them back out the door.

"Girl space and you're invading it. Later," she said to her brothers.

"Oh, come on," said Chad. "We were downstairs trying to make egg salad sandwiches to take to school tomorrow and realized we're fresh out of eggs. Think we could borrow a half dozen until the next grocery run?"

Stevie let out a loud distressed howl and ran back to the incubator, standing protectively between it and her brothers. Then she burst into tears.

Chad, Alex, and Michael looked mystified.

Lisa and Carole were confused, too, *What in the world is wrong with Stevie?* Lisa wondered. If this was indeed Stevie. And she wasn't at all sure that the girl standing in front of her, sobbing helplessly, *was* Stevie Lake simply because the *real* Stevie Lake would have instantly descended upon her brothers with a fierce, warriorlike battle cry. The sound Stevie made was more like that of a drowning cat.

"Hey, we were only kidding," Alex said cautiously.

Chad looked just as uncertain as Alex about how to respond. "It's okay, Stevie. Alex is right. We didn't mean it. There are still plenty of eggs in the fridge," he said awkwardly, apparently not realizing he'd made things worse until Stevie's sobbing turned into a wail. Chad sneaked a glance at Lisa, who discreetly indicated that they might want to leave the room—fast.

"Ah . . . okay. Um . . . we're going now." Chad made a motion to his brothers to follow him and backed out of the room, quietly closing the door behind them.

Lisa and Carole rushed over and hugged Stevie.

"M-my—my e-eg-eggs . . . ," hiccuped Stevie as she wiped the tears from her cheeks.

"Sssshhhhhhh. They're not going to take your eggs," soothed Carole.

Lisa and Carole exchanged concerned looks over Stevie's shoulder. This wasn't the Stevie they were used to. It certainly wasn't normal for Stevie to be so vulnerable. *Or to be vulnerable at all*, thought Lisa. The only thing she could chalk it up to was the stress of impending motherhood. Or goosehood. Or whatever it was called.

Slowly, Stevie's tears subsided. She brushed the dampness off her cheeks. "I'm okay now. Thanks." She smiled at her friends. "You guys should probably be getting home."

Carole glanced at her watch and realized Stevie was right. "I promised Dad I'd be back for dinner."

Lisa gave Stevie an extra hug for comfort then headed to the bedroom door with Carole. "Remember," she said, "we'll be working on vaulting in Tuesday's class."

Stevie nodded.

Lisa's and Carole's voices slowly faded as they made

their way down the stairs, buzzing again about the upcoming vaulting class. Stevie got to her feet and quietly closed her bedroom door. Then she crossed the room and pulled a pillow and synthetic comforter off the bed. She curled up on the carpet next to the incubator and snuggled under the blanket, keeping a watchful eye on her eggs.

TUESDAY'S VAULTING LESSON couldn't come soon enough, as far as the girls were concerned. Max had promised his students that they would finally get a chance to try a couple of simple moves on Clara. Almost every other word that had come out of Lisa's or Carole's mouth since Sunday had had something to do with vaulting. Not that Stevie wasn't just as excited, but she was also quite preoccupied with her eggs and was finding it difficult to concentrate on anything else.

Lisa glanced down at her dance tights. "I feel like I showed up for the wrong lesson," she joked.

Carole and Stevie, who were also wearing tights instead of their standard riding breeches, had to agree.

Max had instructed everyone to wear snug, flexible clothing for the day's lesson. Although breeches were ideal for riding, they weren't as suitable for vaulting.

"Wait until you try walking across the arena floor in these," said Stevie, pulling on a pair of soft-soled, ballet-like slippers that Max had also requested they wear so that they wouldn't injure Clara's back.

The first part of the class had been a repeat of Sunday's ground exercises, followed by some work on the barrel for balance. When Max was satisfied that everyone had taken a turn, he'd told them to quickly change their footwear and meet him in the indoor arena.

The girls arrived in the arena to see Red already warming up Clara on the longe line. It was the first time Stevie had seen the large mare work, and she had to admit that Clara looked quite impressive decked out in her vaulting gear. She was outfitted in a simple snaffle bit. Side reins ran from the bit to the vaulting surcingle. The surcingle itself consisted of a large thick belt of padded leather, approximately eight inches wide, that wrapped around Clara's withers and belly and was buckled up on either side, very similar to a saddle girth. Along the top of the surcingle were two leather-covered handles. Cossack straps were attached below the handles on either side, which Stevie suspected would be used to help the shorter riders mount. Between the surcingle and Clara's back was a thick cotton pad. Red had also wrapped Clara's lower legs for added support.

Red clucked softly to Clara and the large mare instantly shifted from a trot into a canter. Stevie, Lisa, and Carole watched in awe at the sight of Clara cantering in a perfect circle around Red. Her stride was so even and balanced that she appeared to float above the ground.

"Wow . . . I wish Belle were that smooth," Stevie whispered.

The soft ground beneath the girls' feet shook as all 1,400 pounds of Clara cantered past. So she didn't exactly float, mused Stevie.

"One of the most important things in vaulting," Max began, "is the soft arena. Not only does it protect Clara's legs from injury, but it also protects the vaulters from landing on too hard of a surface if they fall off."

"You mean 'when'," corrected Stevie.

Max smiled and continued. "The other important thing is to make sure that the horse is properly warmed up. And because a vaulting horse spends most of its time working in a circle, it's necessary to cross train with other disciplines, such as dressage or jumping, to maximize muscle development and flexibility. Students aren't the only ones who need to be flexible in vaulting."

The class laughed at Max's comment as Red slowed Clara to a walk.

"So who wants to go first?" Max asked brightly. The riders looked at each other. "What about you, Carole?" he suggested.

Carole nodded and stepped forward. Ordinarily all three of The Saddle Club girls would have volunteered to go first, but this time they were all just a little nervous.

While Red longed Clara at a walk, Max boosted Carole gently onto the mare's back. Max had already explained to them that the Vault-on, which was how vaulters mounted their horses at the canter, was a more difficult move and would come later in the training. Besides that, a Vault-on was never performed at a walk because there wasn't enough momentum to swing the rider onto the horse's back without putting stress on the horse's shoulder and leg muscles.

"She feels like a giant rocking chair!" Carole exclaimed excitedly, instantly forgetting her nervousness. She adjusted her seat on Clara's broad back, enjoying the even tempo of the mare's walk. Instinctively she reached up to adjust her helmet, then remembered she wasn't wearing one. She grinned at Max. "It's like getting into a car and not putting your seat belt on."

Max nodded. "It'll take a little bit of getting used to."

It was the first time that Carole could think of that Max had actually instructed the students *not* to wear their helmets. As Max had explained to them, helmets could interfere with balance and peripheral vision. It was especially important in the more advanced moves, where vaulters rested their heads directly against the horse's body for stability. The interference of a helmet could cause them to slip and fall.

"All right, Carole, let's begin with the Basic Seat."

The Basic Seat was easy—it was no different than a similar exercise that Max had them do in regular mounted classes. Carole extended her arms at shoulder level and looked straight ahead. She stretched her legs down, squeezing slightly so that no light shone between her legs and Clara's sides.

"Very good," said Max. "Now, I want you to gently swing your legs forward and then back, bringing yourself up to a kneeling position on Clara's back."

The students watched, captivated, as Carole gripped the handles of the vaulting surcingle and followed Max's instructions, timing her movements with the slow, even, four-beat tempo of Clara's walk.

"The next thing we're going to try is an up-to-the-knees, which is basically a half Stand. Pretty soon you'll be able to do these moves at the canter," said Max. "In a way it will be easier because of the tempo. But I want to make sure that everyone gets a feel for the positions before we try that."

Max walked along beside Clara, coaching Carole as she moved from a kneeling position into a crouched position, bringing one foot up first and then the other. Carole tried to let go of the handles and immediately lost her balance, slipping awkwardly to the side.

"Don't forget your emergency dismount," reminded Max.

Carole quickly swung both her legs over Clara's rump and landed in the soft arena dirt, rolling over her shoulder to lessen the impact. "Very good, Carole," said Max.

Stevie was next. She was surprised at how difficult it was to keep her balance once she let go of the handles. Before she knew it, she found herself sitting in the dirt off to the side of the longeing circle, watching Clara's large black-and-white rump as the horse sauntered past. Clara glanced back curiously as if to say, "What are you doing down there?"

Lisa didn't fare much better. She slowly picked herself up off the ground, brushing at the arena dirt on her clothes, wondering how on earth anyone actually managed to stay on the horse.

"Max, there's no way we're going to be able to learn how to do this in a month," announced Meg, one of the other students in the class who had also fallen off shortly after mounting.

"At this rate we'll be lucky to learn it in a year," declared Stevie, quite frustrated with the way the lesson was progressing—or rather, not progressing. What was bothering her the most, besides the obvious fact that she'd fallen off, was that she suddenly felt like a total beginner again. And she could see from the frowns on the other students' faces that they were feeling exactly the same way.

Max seemed unconcerned, even though no one in the class had managed to stay on for more than a few strides in any position other than the Basic Seat. "It's like riding a bicycle," he said. "These exercises aren't any different from the ones you did on the barrel. You just need to get used to the feel of the 'moving floor' underneath you."

Stevie thought Max's comment seemed odd, especially since they were all very used to the feel of a horse's motion.

"Come on, let's give it another try," Max said encouragingly.

Everyone lined up. The Saddle Club girls exchanged surprised looks as they noticed Veronica, who'd been the least enthusiastic of the bunch to try vaulting in the first place, at the front of the line.

"Maybe she just wants to get it over with," Lisa suggested slowly. "What other logical explanation could there be?"

What surprised the girls even more was that Veronica actually did quite well the second time around, managing to hold the up-to-the-knees position for several strides, her hands out at shoulder level, before falling off.

Determined not to be outdone, Stevie went next. But, again, she lost her balance the moment she released her hold on the handles. And every student after her ended up much the same way. The only other rider who managed to stay on at all was Lisa.

"Use your arms to balance yourself, Lisa," Max reminded her.

Lisa extended her arms, wiggling her toes a little as she balanced her weight evenly between her feet. She slowly rose from the crouched position to the Stand, keeping her knees slightly bent.

"You've got it, Lisa!" Max said excitedly.

Stevie and Carole held their breath as Lisa made it one stride . . . two strides . . . three strides. Lisa wobbled and tipped off to the side, hitting the ground with a graceful roll.

"Nice dismount," said Max.

The class cheered as Lisa leaped to her feet, grinning. That was the longest anyone had managed to stay on.

"That was *sooo* much fun," squealed Lisa, thrilled with her attempt, especially since she hadn't been riding as long as many of the other students in the class. "Three strides! I did three strides!"

"I say we break her kneecaps," teased Stevie. She knew that Lisa's years of ballet and gymnastics were responsible for her agility with the vaulting moves; however, she couldn't help being just a little bit envious.

"Can we have another try?" Carole asked Max. Max nodded.

This time Stevie did a little better. Even though she didn't quite make it into the Stand position, she managed to stay on for several strides before falling off. Lisa continued her standing streak and went half a circle before she needed to grab the handles. This time she didn't fall off.

Veronica went last. Max boosted her onto Clara's back, then stepped back, coaching her as she slowly rose to her feet, her arms extended for balance. "Eyes straight ahead, Veronica. That's it."

Veronica unsteadily held the position for an entire circle. Then her confidence seemed to increase and she relaxed and moved more with Clara's motions. It seemed she was getting a feel for the "moving floor." At Max's nod, she gracefully sat down on Clara's back, then slid off the mare's side, landing on her feet.

"Excellent, Veronica," praised Max.

Stevie gagged, quickly covering up with a small coughing fit when she noticed Max's disapproving look.

Max turned to the class. "I think that's enough for one day. Good work, everyone."

"Good? I think we need to get him glasses," Stevie said to Lisa and Carole. "Since the only one who was any good at all was Lisa." She noticed Veronica approaching. "Oh . . . and her," she added grudgingly.

Veronica stopped beside Stevie, smoothing the wrinkles out of her shirt. "You know, I think that mare has some fine breeding in her," she commented. "Clydesdale, perhaps. Maybe Percheron." She glanced back at Clara, watching as Red brought the mare to a halt, completely missing the stunned look on Stevie's face.

Fine breeding? thought Stevie. *Miss Veronica diAngelo who only rides expensive purebreds thinks that ordinary old Clara has fine breeding?* It was too much for her. She reached out and touched Veronica's forehead. "Do you think she has a fever?" She asked Lisa and Carole.

Veronica impatiently brushed Stevie's hand aside. "Just because *you* couldn't stay on doesn't mean that *Clara* doesn't know what she's doing. Only an impeccably bred horse could possess the qualities that Clara displayed today."

Max's lips twitched in amusement at Veronica's very un-Veronica-like comment. "I can assure you, Veronica, Clara's just a good old workhorse with a smooth gait."

"That's what I'm saying," continued Veronica. "Look at her stride. Her movement. That sort of quality only comes from fine breeding."

"You're only saying that because Clara let you stay on," Stevie blurted out.

Veronica smiled at Stevie, sugar sweet. "We all rode the same horse. Besides, you know what they say: It's not the horse, it's the rider. And I guess some riders just have more talent than others."

Stevie bristled, feeling ready to breathe fire in Veronica's direction.

"Max, do you think you could give me some extra balancing exercises that I could practice at home this week?" Veronica continued.

Now it was Max's turn to look shocked. Veronica wasn't typically one to show initiative. And certainly not when it required work. "Ah . . . sure," he responded.

"Good," said Veronica. She turned on her heel, making her way out of the arena.

After class, Stevie, Lisa, and Carole helped cool out

Clara, then checked on their own horses before getting ready to go home. They were hoping to walk together so that they could talk more about Veronica, but Carole's father, Colonel Hanson, was waiting in the car when they came out of the barn.

"Hi, girls," said Colonel Hanson.

"Hey, Colonel Hanson," answered Lisa and Stevie in unison.

Carole said good-bye to Stevie and Lisa before settling into her dad's car.

As the vehicle pulled down the drive, Lisa and Stevie followed at a leisurely walk. It took Stevie only a moment to get onto the hot topic of the day: Veronica.

"After all her talk about *not* wanting to stand on a horse's back, I can't believe she did so well," said Stevie. "In fact, it's sickening."

"I can't believe how much fun that was!" Lisa said, still thinking about her first experience with vaulting.

Stevie scowled at Lisa, who obviously didn't understand the importance of the whole Veronica vaulting catastrophe. "Fun? Lisa, don't you get it? If Veronica suddenly becomes interested in vaulting, she might actually do *well* at the competition at the end of the month."

Lisa frowned. She hadn't thought of that.

"We have to do better than she does," Stevie stressed quite dramatically. "We can't let her win. And you're our only hope. You're the only one who can beat Veronica."

"I don't know, Stevie," Lisa responded skeptically. "Veronica did pretty well today."

"So did you!" Stevie assured her. "Lisa, you're a natural. All you have to do now is practice like crazy."

Stevie had a point. Lisa did have the advantage of her ballet training. She just had to learn how to apply it to vaulting. "Okay, I'll do it. I'll beat Veronica," declared Lisa.

Stevie smiled. "That's the spirit. Now you go practice, while I check on my eggs."

STEVIE ARRIVED HOME, passing her mother as she came out of the kitchen.

"Stevie," Mrs. Lake called out, "there are fresh brownies on the counter and milk in the—"

"Later, Mom," Stevie said hurriedly as she turned the corner and took the stairs two at a time up to her bedroom. Never in her life had she passed on fresh brownies and milk, but she had more important things to do today.

Upstairs, Stevie burst into her room and ran straight to the incubator. True to her word, her mother had turned the eggs on schedule, as well as checked it off on Stevie's "Egg-Turning Wall Chart" that Lisa had made to keep Stevie organized. The chart was incredibly detailed, listing the required incubator temperatures, turning times, and routine egg checks. According to the chart, Stevie could stop turning her eggs on Wednesday, which was the next day. The eggs wouldn't need to be turned for the last few days of their incubation period.

Satisfied that everything was in order, Stevie plunked herself down at her desk and opened her algebra book. She had an assignment due the next day that she'd kept putting off because of her distraction with the eggs. Now seemed like a good time to get it out of the way.

Stevie grabbed a pencil and carefully wrote out an algebra equation, her eyes straying periodically to the incubator before returning to the page. As she attempted to solve the problem, she caught herself staring at the zero she'd jotted. She'd outlined it several times, causing it to take on an oval shape—like a goose egg. She gave the algebra equation several more attempts, but it was no use. Algebra reminded her too much of her eggs.

Stevie figured that perhaps it was the type of homework she was doing. Maybe if she worked on something without zeros, it would be easier to concentrate.

And, unfortunately, she had plenty of other homework she could do. History, for instance. Their teacher had hinted at the possibility of a pop quiz on Napoleon's retreat from Moscow. But reading the text automatically triggered thoughts of how cold it must have been in Moscow, and Stevie wondered if Napoleon used a goose-down comforter.

Realizing it was happening again, Stevie closed the history book and pulled out her English assignment. Her class was reading *Animal Farm*. Stevie tried really, really hard to concentrate, but the mention of all the animals was very distracting. It was absolutely, positively hopeless.

Stevie didn't understand how any teacher could expect her to do homework with something as exciting as impending motherhood. Plus, she hadn't looked at the eggs for nearly five minutes and was starting to feel like she was neglecting them. Resigned to the fact that concentration wasn't something that was going to happen anytime soon, she closed her book and returned to her new favorite spot: in front of the incubator.

Stevie was adjusting her pillow when, out of the corner of her eye, she thought she caught a movement in the incubator. But when she looked again, all twelve eggs were resting comfortably, no sign of activity. She peered closely at the eggs, holding her breath, but nothing happened. Not even the slightest wiggle. But she was sure she'd seen *something*.

Without taking her eyes off the eggs for a second, Stevie reached for the phone, tugging on the cord to draw it toward her. She quickly dialed Lisa's number and waited breathlessly while the phone rang.

"Hello?" answered Lisa.

"You're not going to believe this," Stevie said in a rush. "I think it moved!"

"An egg?" Lisa guessed.

"Of course an egg," Stevie said excitedly. With the receiver cradled against one shoulder, she reached for the literature that had accompanied the eggs. She flipped through it, looking for some kind of prehatching symptoms.

"The little fellow was probably just getting comfortable in there," Lisa suggested. "I wouldn't worry about it."

Not worry about it? Stevie wasn't sure what response she'd expected from Lisa, but it wasn't that. She quickly ran her index finger down each page as she skimmed the text. There was information on absolutely everything from breed types to suggested care instructions. But she couldn't find anything on egg wiggling. Not that the egg did wiggle for sure. But what if it had?

Lisa, who obviously didn't understand the possible significance of a wiggling egg, had already changed topics and was going on about her new favorite subject: vaulting.

"I'm completely psyched about the competition," Lisa said excitedly. "I even stopped at the bookstore on the way home and picked up a book on vaulting. I've been practicing some of the moves and I want to try them on Clara. At the walk anyway. There's the Basic Seat and the Stand, which we already kind of tried. But there's also the Flag and the Mill. If we were entering a real competition, we'd also need to be able to perform the Vault-on, the Scissors, and the Flank." She paused to catch her breath and suddenly realized that Stevie hadn't made so much as a peep on the other end of the line. "Uh . . . Stevie?"

Stevie gasped.

Lisa frowned. "Stevie?" There was no response. "Stevie, what's going on?"

Lisa heard another gasp at the other end of the line, this time louder.

"Stevie!" shouted Lisa, worried.

There was a dull thunk as the phone dropped from

Stevie's hand and hit a hard surface. It was followed by a dial tone as the line went dead.

Lisa frantically jumped to her feet, running out of her bedroom. She rushed down the stairs, shoved her feet into a worn pair of sneakers, and grabbed a jacket as she raced out the front door.

LISA DIDN'T LIVE far from Stevie's house. She ran the entire way, panicked that something had happened to one of her best friends. It was just after eight-thirty, and she wasn't usually allowed out this time of the evening on a school night, but she figured that if Stevie was in trouble, that was all the excuse she needed for a fast exit.

Lisa cut across the Lakes' front lawn and banged on the front door. A moment later it was opened by Mrs. Lake. "Lisa, what on earth are you doing here at this hour—"

"Something's happened to Stevie," Lisa blurted out, trying to catch her breath. "We were on the phone and it suddenly went dead."

Concerned, Mrs. Lake and Lisa ran up the stairs to Stevie's bedroom. Without bothering to knock, they burst into the room.

"Shhh," Stevie hushed them, and then waved her hand, inviting them to join her.

"Stevie, are you—" Mrs. Lake stopped short at the sight before them.

Stevie was hovering over the incubator, her expression full of awe. One of the eggs was definitely wiggling. Mrs. Lake and Lisa crept up beside Stevie, quietly taking a seat on the carpet beside the incubator to watch.

"How long has it been doing that?" Lisa whispered.

"At least five minutes," Stevie answered quietly. "It started out with just a little wiggle, and now it won't sit still."

"Then it definitely takes after Stevie," Mrs. Lake teased.

"Do you think it needs any help?" asked Lisa, concerned.

Stevie shook her head. "The instructions said not to touch it unless it gets stuck coming out of the shell."

Lisa, Stevie, and Mrs. Lake all gasped as a small, thin crack made its way along the top of the shell.

Stevie squealed in delight. "It's hatching! It's hatching!"

A moment later Mr. Lake popped his head through

the bedroom doorway. "I heard the screaming," he said. "What's going on up here?"

"One of Stevie's eggs is hatching," Lisa answered excitedly.

Intrigued, Mr. Lake entered the room and peered over Mrs. Lake's shoulder. "Well, look at that," he said, smiling.

As if just realizing they were missing out on a big event, Stevie's brothers came pounding up the stairs and burst into the bedroom.

"Are they hatching?" Alex asked loudly.

Stevie quickly put her finger to her lips. "Shushhh! You might scare them."

Obediently, Alex made his way over to the incubator. He hunched down quietly on the carpet beside Stevie and Lisa. Chad and Michael followed, respectfully keeping silent, their mouths shaped in small o's as they watched the hairline crack in the egg lengthen.

"Once they're born," Stevie explained, "I'll transfer them to the brooder." She indicated the brooder that had come in a kit with the eggs. It was a wooden box about two feet long and eighteen inches high. Stevie had carefully mounted two 40-watt lightbulbs to the top of the box at one end. "The heat from the lightbulbs will keep the goslings warm for the first few weeks until they're able to take care of themselves," she explained.

In the bottom of the box, Stevie had spread several layers of newspaper, covered with a couple of old bath towels that Mrs. Lake had kindly donated to the Mother Goose Project. The bath towels would provide traction for the newborn goslings so that they wouldn't slip and hurt themselves. Stevie had read that the wrong type of footing could permanently damage the fragile legs of the newborns.

"How long is this going to ta—" Michael's sentence was cut short as the eggshell suddenly cracked open at the top and a tiny yellow beak popped out.

"Eyes! I can see eyes," Lisa whispered excitedly.

The egg wiggled again. The hole in the shell became larger. They could now see that the tiny yellow beak was attached to an equally tiny grayish yellow head. Stevie grasped Lisa's hand and held on tightly, resisting the urge to reach into the incubator and help the little thing along.

Finally, just before ten o'clock, the first gosling emerged.

"You're beautiful," Stevie murmured to the gosling, awed.

"I don't know if it's *beautiful*," Alex said skeptically. "It's kind of wet and scrawny looking. And it's gray."

The gosling took a step, stumbled, then slowly regained its balance. It looked around at the other eggs, a few of which were also now starting to wiggle. The little gosling glared at Stevie and honked.

"Okay, little one, I get the message. You want to come out." Stevie carefully lifted the lid on the incubator. Ever so gently, she reached inside and picked up the gosling. It was warm and damp and felt odd in Stevie's hand. It was so light that she could hardly believe it was real, until it honked again, this time louder and with more determination.

Stevie held the tiny newborn up to her face to examine it closely. What she found was that it could match her stare for stare—clearly as curious about her as she was about it. It honked insistently.

"All right, all right," answered Stevie, placing the gosling carefully in the brooder. "You're a bossy one. No wonder you were born first."

She added a small tray of feed to the brooder, close enough to the gosling that he wouldn't have to stumble too far to reach it. Chad volunteered to get some water and shortly returned with a shallow dish, which Stevie placed a few inches from the food. "There you go, Number One," said Stevie. Number One honked again and popped his beak into the feed, experimenting. Before they knew it, he was eating and drinking, quite literally at the same time. He filled his beak with food then took a mouthful of water, dropping some of the food on the towel in his haste to drink.

"You may need to speak to him about his table manners," teased Lisa.

Stevie smiled. She thought Number One was so cute, she could easily overlook the fact that he was a bit of a pig. Besides, she doubted that she had been the neatest eater when she was little.

Having had his fill, Number One waddled a few inches from the feed tray, shook himself off, and then collapsed into a fluffy little ball of feathers. Moments later he was sound asleep.

"So much for that," said Stevie.

"On that note," said Mrs. Lake, "I think that we should do the same."

The boys groaned, but Mrs. Lake reminded everyone that despite the special occasion, it was still a school night.

As the boys slowly left the room, Mr. Lake turned to Lisa. "Come on, I'll walk you home."

"Make sure you get some sleep tonight," Lisa said to Stevie on her way out the door.

Stevie smiled, watching as her father followed Lisa and her mother down the stairs. Moments later, she heard the click of the front door.

Stevie took a last look at the incubator. Everything was peaceful and still. She pulled on her pajamas and crawled into bed, satisfied that the eggs and Number One were all doing fine. Then she reached out and turned off the lamp beside her bed.

LISA CRAWLED INTO bed and snuggled under the covers, checking her alarm clock to make sure it was set. She closed her eyes to sleep but was too overwhelmed by what she'd seen earlier.

Of course, she, Stevie, and Carole had experienced the miracle of birth before. They'd watched Delilah's foal, Samson, be born. And the cats at the stable were always having kittens. But this was different. The little creature had had to fight so hard to break the shell to get into the world. Lisa found it absolutely amazing. With her thoughts on Number One, she drifted off into a contented sleep.

A FEW HOUSES away, Stevie was finding it a little more difficult to do the same. In the darkness of the room, she thought she could hear movement in the incubator. Perhaps it was Number Two trying to break free.

Stevie glanced at the glowing numbers on the clock. It was 10:35—eight and a half hours before she'd have to get up for school. Surely a person didn't need *that* much sleep every night. Stevie decided that if she got up and watched the eggs for just a little longer, she would still have enough time to get plenty of rest before morning. *Besides, how could anyone expect me to sleep at a time like this?* Stevie reasoned.

Her mind made up, Stevie crept out of bed and sat down next to the incubator. The room was dark but the bulbs shining in the brooder provided plenty of light for Stevie to keep an eye on both the incubator and Number One, whose feathers had begun to dry under the gentle heat of the light.

Stevie turned her attention to the incubator. Sure enough, as she had suspected, Number Two was wiggling madly away, attempting to break out of its shell. And another egg, Number Three, had also decided it was time to hatch. However, neither of the eggs appeared to be in any great rush.

Stevie grabbed her pillow and comforter off the bed and snuggled down on the floor beside the incubator. She rested her head on her pillow, watching the eggs as they wiggled purposefully. Her eyelids grew heavy, even as she struggled to keep them open. She was determined to be awake when the goslings were born. That was the last thought Stevie had before she drifted off to sleep.

Stevie was jerked awake by the frantic quacking of Number Two, who seemed a little perturbed that she had slept through his entire birth. He glared at Stevie and impatiently quacked again until she sleepily got to her knees and lifted the lid off the incubator.

"Breakfast is coming," she said softly, moving him to the brooder and placing him gently beside Number One, who had awakened to greet his sibling. Stevie was watching Number One show Two how to eat when she suddenly heard another quack behind her—Number Three!

Stevie scooped him up and placed him in the brooder beside One and Two. Then she quietly opened her bedroom door and tiptoed down the hall to get fresh water from the bathroom sink. When she returned, goslings One through Three had already finished off the feed. Stevie added more, along with the water, then watched until they'd had their fill. Then the three little goslings cuddled together and promptly fell asleep.

Stevie tiredly rubbed her eyes as she glanced at the clock. It was two A.M.! Five more hours and it would be time to get up for school—which no longer gave her very much time to sleep. Stevie picked up her pillow and comforter and gratefully crawled back into bed.

Stevie was awakened a few hours later by another persistent quack. Number Four was staring at Stevie, apparently waiting to be added to the brooder with his other siblings. "I'm coming, I'm coming," mumbled Stevie, stumbling out of bed yet again and finding her way to the incubator. She picked up Number Four and put him in with Numbers One through Three.

Feeling that she should stay awake so as not to miss any more of the hatchings, Stevie once again grabbed her pillow and comforter. This time she settled into her armchair, propping her head up with her pillow. No sooner had she shut her eyes than an annoying *beep, beep, beep* pulled her out of her stupor.

"Number Five," she mumbled. "I'm coming." The beeping continued, and Stevie opened one eye. The room was flooded with sunlight. The noise wasn't Number Five, it was her alarm clock. "It can't be morning already," she groaned. She felt as if she hadn't slept a wink.

Stevie wiggled her toes and was surprised to find something warm and fuzzy resting on them. Curious, she leaned forward and glanced down at her feet, which were poking out from under the comforter. Numbers One and Three had somehow managed to escape from the brooder and were snuggled up against her bare feet, fast asleep. Stevie smiled, suddenly feeling very maternal. After all, what was a little lost sleep?

9

STEVIE WAS NOT having a good day at school. After putting One and Three back in the brooder, she'd rushed to get ready for school, running out the door while still trying to tie her shoelaces. Taking care of the quacking little goslings (all of whom had made her very aware that they preferred to be fed *immediately* upon rising) had made Stevie late leaving the house, which meant that she hadn't had time to call Carole and tell her that four of the goslings had hatched. She'd also forgotten to grab breakfast, which caused her stomach to growl uncomfortably all through history class. To make matters worse, not only had she not done her homework for that day's classes, but she'd also forgotten her algebra book at home on her desk, which meant that she'd had to ask her teacher if she could share with another student. Her teacher was not pleased.

The only class Stevie felt awake in was the last class of the day, science. The class was doing a unit on biology. Ms. Anderson had begun the hour with a discussion of the anatomy of an earthworm, a subject that was totally revolting to Stevie. She had far too many gruesome memories of what her brothers liked to do to earthworms. Alex's favorite experiment was to see how many earthworms he could make out of one.

Stevie raised her hand.

"Yes, Stevie?" said Ms. Anderson.

In hopes of deterring her teacher from the current discussion, Stevie explained about the goose eggs that she'd won in the Job's Comforters contest and how they'd started to hatch the night before.

Intrigued, Ms. Anderson agreed to momentarily put aside the discussion of the earthworm to allow Stevie to tell the class about her eggs. Stevie made her way to the front of the room and used the chalkboard to draw diagrams of the eggs, the incubator, and the brooder as she spoke. Unfortunately, once you've described one gosling hatching, you've basically described them all, despite Stevie's attempts at creative storytelling. Even with the question-and-answer period, she was only able to stretch her egg discussion to ten minutes.

"Thank you, Stevie," said Ms. Anderson as Stevie took her seat again. There was still half an hour of class left, and, much to the students' dismay, their teacher quickly returned to the earthworm's finer internal points.

Veronica, sitting two rows over from Stevie, had faked several yawns throughout Stevie's lecture on goose eggs, wearing a look that clearly said, *Could anything be more boring?* Unfortunately, the answer was yes. Earthworms. And Veronica seemed to have even less of an urge to listen to *that* topic than she did to Stevie's ramblings about wiggling eggs.

"Okay, everyone, please turn to page two-fifty-six for a picture of the earthworm's anatomy," said Ms. Anderson.

As the students dutifully turned to the proper page, Veronica scooped up her books, got to her feet, and walked to the front of the class. "I'd love to stay for the rest of what is likely to be a very interesting discussion," she said sweetly to Ms. Anderson, "but I have to go." She handed the teacher a note. "I have an important appointment." With the assumption that permission had already been granted, she turned and left the class, shooting Stevie an overly sweet smile on her way out the door.

Joe Novick, who sat next to Stevie, leaned over. "You'd think people as rich as the diAngelos could get orthodontists to make house calls," he joked.

Stevie shook her head disgustedly and shrugged.

Overhearing Joe's remark, Ms. Anderson smiled, amused, and glanced at the note. "Well, it's not an orthodontist's appointment. It's her—" The teacher squinted, apparently not believing what she was reading. "It's her vaulting coach."

Stevie gagged. She should have known that Veronica would pull a stunt like that. Especially since her sudden interest the other day. And especially since she wasn't one to take competitions lightly, even schooling competitions at Pine Hollow. Stevie had to warn Lisa and Carole.

The remainder of the class seemed to take forever. The more impatient Stevie got, the slower the class went. An eternity later, the bell finally sounded, signaling the end of class and the school day.

Stevie shoved her books in her locker and dashed over to Pine Hollow, where she was certain she would find Lisa and Carole. She was not disappointed.

Stevie found everyone at the outdoor ring, where

Lisa and Carole, along with several other students, were taking turns practicing their skills on Clara. Red was again acting as the longeur, as well as calling out tips to the riders. Max stood at the fence, watching, pleased to see the progress his students were making.

"Hey, Stevie, you're just in time," said Lisa as Stevie rushed up to them. "Max said we could practice our vaulting today."

Stevie bent over and rested her hands on her knees, waving her arm as she tried to catch her breath from her quick dash to the stable. "Can't stay . . . have to hurry home . . . no time . . ."

Lisa and Carole exchanged looks.

"Where's the fire?" joked Carole.

Stevie shook her head. She gulped for breath. "Goslings . . ."

"*Lings?*" asked Lisa, surprised. "As in more than one?"

This time Stevie nodded. "Four," she managed to say, holding up four fingers to emphasize the point.

"The eggs hatched last night?" asked Carole, incredulous.

Lisa smiled guiltily. She'd been so excited about getting to their vaulting practice that she'd completely forgotten to mention the eggs. "I was on the phone with Stevie last night when they started hatching," she told Carole. "Only Stevie—being Stevie—instead of telling me what was going on, led me to believe that she'd just had a heart attack, or worse, and then she hung up on me."

"To be fair," interrupted Stevie as she straightened up, slowly regaining her breath, "that was definitely a 'they're hatching' type of gasp, and I didn't hang up on you, I dropped the phone."

"So when the phone crashed to the floor," continued Lisa dramatically, "I thought I should run over to make sure that one of my best friends hadn't accidentally suffered a concussion executing a nosedive out of her desk chair. But instead of finding her unconscious on the floor, I found her hovering over the incubator like an anxious parent-to-be."

"I wasn't hovering," Stevie replied indignantly. "I was being *aware*."

"Well, that was the most aware I've ever seen you," Lisa teased.

"What about the rest of the eggs?" Carole asked.

"I don't know. I've got to get home and see if more have hatched." She explained to Carole that she'd been numbering the goslings in the order they were born. "It'll have to do until I can come up with proper names for them," she added.

"How are you ever going to keep them straight once they've all hatched?" Carole asked curiously.

"No problem—or not so far, anyway," said Stevie. "Number One is very bossy and loud. And Number Four's quack has a different pitch. Two has this flutter thing that he does with his wings, and Three has more colors in his feathers than any of the others."

"See, she already sounds like a mom," said Lisa.

"Well, seeing as I missed the big event," said Carole, "you'll have to tell me all about it. I think it's so exciting that you're a mom!"

"It is, and I have to get back. But I didn't come to tell you about the goslings. Well, I did, but there's something else. You're absolutely not going to believe this," said Stevie, pausing for effect. "Veronica got out of class early today because she had an appointment with her *vaulting* coach."

"Vaulting coach?" echoed Lisa and Carole, incredulous.

"We've gotta do something!" said Stevie. "And I'll figure out what as soon as I get home and take care of the eggs. Goslings. Goslings and eggs. Gotta go!"

Stevie dashed off before the news had even finished sinking in.

"Stevie, wait!" shouted Carole.

But Stevie had disappeared through the door and Carole realized she was probably halfway down the driveway already, headed home to her waiting goslings.

Carole turned to Lisa, her expression serious. "Well, that's it then. You've just got to win for us."

Lisa sighed and watched as one of the students struggled with the Stand. The two riders after that didn't fare much better. Finally it was Lisa's turn.

Lisa slipped gracefully onto Clara's back, grasping the handles for support until she'd adjusted her seat and was moving easily with Clara's even stride. She extended her arms out to either side and stretched her legs toward the ground.

"Raise your arms a little higher, Lisa," Max reminded her. "That's it."

Lisa raised her arms slightly and remembered to keep her eyes forward, looking between Clara's ears.

"When you're ready," said Red, "move into the Flag."

Lisa nodded. It was one of the moves that she'd been practicing at home and she thought she had a pretty good idea of how to do it. Grabbing the handles on the surcingle, she adjusted her position so that she was kneeling on Clara's back. Then she raised her right leg until it was straight back and her left arm until it was straight in front.

"Very good," praised Red. "Now let's go into the Stand."

Grasping the surcingle handles, Lisa pulled her knees beneath her, then moved into a squatting position on Clara's back. She shifted her weight in time to Clara's movements.

Then she released the handles, feeling the stride for a moment before slowly rising to a standing position. She did two full circles at the Stand before Red nodded.

Max approached. "That was very good, Lisa. Go back into the Basic Seat and we'll try it at the canter."

Lisa gently lowered herself into the Basic Seat, experiencing a strange mix of nervousness and excitement. It wasn't as if she'd never cantered before. She'd just never tried it while standing up.

Max glanced over at Carole. "Carole, why don't you give us a hand?"

Carole came forward. Lisa was confused. How was Carole going to help? Her question was answered when Max boosted her onto Clara's back in front of the surcingle, facing Lisa. The girls smiled nervously.

"All right Lisa, when you go into the Stand, I want you to hold on to Carole's shoulders for support. Carole, I want you to hold on to Lisa's legs." The girls nodded. "Once you're comfortable, Lisa, extend your arms to the side and Carole will help you balance."

Lisa nodded.

Red clucked softly to Clara, and before the girls even realized that they'd changed stride, Clara was moving with the rocking three-beat motion of the canter. Lisa couldn't believe how smooth it was!

Max smiled at the surprise he saw on Lisa's face. "A vaulting horse's stride is second only to its temperament."

Even though Clara's stride was smoother than any canter she'd ever sat to, Lisa still found herself bouncing slightly with the movement.

"Relax your lower back, Lisa," Max reminded her.

It was an instruction that Max gave often when they were riding. Lisa knew that a stiff back prevented her from properly feeling the motion of the horse. She took a deep breath, relaxing the muscles in her back as she exhaled. The moment she did so, she noticed a difference in her seat.

"Are you ready to try the Stand at the canter?" asked Max.

Lisa made a face. She was definitely ready to try it. Whether or not she could actually do it was another matter.

As if reading her thoughts, Carole smiled and whispered, "You can do it, Lisa."

Gripping Carole's shoulders, Lisa slowly moved into the Stand. When she felt balanced, she released her hold on Carole and extended her arms to the sides. She made it an entire circle at the center before she lost her balance. She quickly returned to the Basic Seat, holding on to Carole's shoulders for support as she lowered herself gently onto Clara's back.

"That was great!" Carole said.

Lisa smiled, knowing that she'd done much better than she had at her last lesson, but she highly doubted it would be enough to beat Veronica now that she had her own private vaulting coach.

"Okay, Carole, you're up," said Max.

Lisa hopped off to allow Carole to go through the same vaulting moves she had done. Lisa watched attentively, silently cheering her friend on as she went through the same routine at a walk.

"That was great," she said when Carole dismounted and joined her at the edge of the ring.

"I think that's good for today," Max said. "Who brought the treats?" The riders immediately moved forward to give Clara thank-you pats and a few pieces of carrot. Clara lapped up the attention, enjoying her queenly status.

In exchange for being able to ride Clara, all the students were required to help take care of the large mare, before and after class. That included a rubdown, mucking out her stall, providing fresh hay and water, and cleaning her tack so that it would be ready for the next lesson.

The riders split the duties equally among them, rotating with each lesson to make sure that everyone got a chance to do the more favorable chores, such as bathing Clara, as well as the not-so-favorable chores, such as mucking out her stall.

Today it was Lisa and Carole's turn to make sure that Clara was properly cooled out. After pulling off the equipment, they led her to the wash stall and hooked her up to the cross-ties. They readied their sponges and buckets, then simply stared at Clara's huge head, which was several feet above theirs.

"I think we're going to need a ladder," Lisa joked.

But the moment Lisa lifted her arm, Clara gently lowered her head, allowing Lisa to reach the top of her neck. The mare sighed contentedly as Lisa swept the cool sponge down the length of her sweaty neck.

Lisa laughed. "I think she likes this."

When they'd finished bathing her, the girls relaxed by leaning against the mare's stall, contemplating Clara's shiny coat. Clara returned their gazes and nickered her thanks.

Carole smiled and said, "I wish we had more time to practice. It's going to be pretty tough to beat Veronica now."

"You're probably right," Lisa said. Once Veronica set her mind to something, nothing would stand in her way. And certainly not anything as meager as the expense of hiring a private coach.

"Well," said Lisa, trying to look on the positive side, "we have something that she doesn't."

"What's that?" asked Carole, confused. She couldn't think of anything that Veronica didn't have.

"We have Clara," said Lisa, smiling.

"You're absolutely right," Carole agreed. "Wherever Veronica is taking her lessons, she can't possibly have as great a horse as Clara."

As if understanding Carole's words, Clara nickered and nuzzled the top of her head. The girls laughed, reaching up on tiptoe to hug the mare's thick neck.

MEANWHILE, BACK AT Stevie's house, two more goslings had hatched and were impatiently waiting to be fed.

"Five and Six," said Stevie. "Okay, you guys—or girls . . ." She paused, realizing she had no idea what sex the goslings were. That would have to wait until she knew a little more about the anatomy of a goose. To be safe, she settled for *little goslings* so as not to offend any of her new charges. "Into your new house, little goslings."

As Stevie opened the incubator to remove Five and Six, she noticed that two more eggs were beginning to wiggle. She placed Five and Six in the brooder, doing a quick check on the goslings that had been born the night before. To her surprise, two were missing. As far as Stevie could tell, it was Numbers One and Three—the same two that had escaped the night before to cuddle up to her feet.

"All right, where have they gone now?" Stevie asked the other goslings. They all stared at her blankly as if to say, *How would we know?*

"A lot of help you guys are," Stevie grumbled good-naturedly. She glanced around her room, wondering where to start. With the pile of clothes in the corner maybe? It looked like a terrific hiding place for young goslings. Stevie crossed the room and lifted up her sweatshirt, only to find a pile of dirty socks beneath it. "Yeeesh." She grimaced. "I guess I should wash those." She quickly replaced the sweatshirt. "*After* I find the two escapees."

Stevie got down on her hands and knees and began looking in the most obvious gosling hiding places—underneath things. Because the goslings were still so small, she doubted that they'd hopped up onto anything. Therefore her search was limited to the floor, which, she thought after taking in the mess on the carpet, was bad enough. It occurred to her that now that she had six (soon to be eight) new little charges, it might make her life easier if she cleaned up her room, especially since they seemed to enjoy playing hide-and-seek.

Stevie crawled along the side of her bed and was just about to peek underneath it when her hand landed in something warm and slippery. She froze, her face crunching up into a disgusted frown.

"Eeeww . . ." Stevie slowly pulled her hand away from the carpet, knowing what she'd find even before she looked. Sure enough, the palm of her hand was stained with the very white, very distinct evidence left behind by either Number One or Number Three. "I see we need to discuss litter training," she announced loudly.

Stevie quickly wiped her hand off on a tissue, cleaned up the remaining mess on the floor, then got back on her knees to continue her search, this time being much more careful about where she put her hands. The droppings did, however, give her a better indication of which direction the little goslings had gone.

Stevie poked her head under the bed. "Ah-hah!" she squealed triumphantly, disturbing Number One, who was comfortably snoozing next to a dust bunny. He was obviously in need of a nap following the afternoon's exciting game of Escape-and-Poop. Stevie gently disengaged the gosling from the dust bunny before returning Number One to the brooder with its siblings.

"Okay, Number Three, where are you hiding?" asked Stevie. She noticed that her closet door was open. "Uh-oh. I hope you're not in there."

Stevie got down on her hands and knees in front of the closet, cringing at the sight that met her eyes. Lisa liked to refer to it as "Stevie's natural disaster area." The inside of the closet resembled more of a going-out-of-business warehouse sale than any kind of repository for clean clothing. The first pile, and the most obvious one for a nap from an escaped gosling's point of view, was littered with the telltale white droppings—obviously calling cards left behind by Number Three. Unfortunately, the droppings didn't indicate where he'd gone after encountering the disaster in the closet.

"He probably ran for his life," chuckled Stevie.

She glanced around and spied the upholstered chair in the corner of her room. The tip of a blue sneaker poked out from behind it. Curious, Stevie crawled across the carpet to the chair, checking underneath her desk as she passed, ensuring that she didn't miss any possible hiding places. She reached the chair and looked behind it. Sure enough, there was Number Three, nestled in the blue sneaker, taking a power snooze.

"Okay, mister, the gig's up," said Stevie, adopting the stern, parental voice that her mom and dad often used when she misbehaved. "Back in the box for you."

Number Three grumbled a bit when she lifted him out of the sneaker, but he didn't bother to open his eyes. In fact, the moment he was in Stevie's hand, he started making himself more comfortable, shifting his feathers around him.

Stevie placed the little gosling in the brooder and checked the others. She seemed to have their undivided attention. All six of them were quietly staring up at her, their eyes filled with adoration.

For a moment Stevie felt herself go weak in the knees, then decided that as their only parental figure she couldn't let something like adorable faces and large dark eyes keep her from making her point.

Stevie sat down cross-legged beside the brooder. "Okay, here's the deal," she said, doing her best to sound stern and parental. "No more day passes from the box. Understood?" Number One blinked, tilting his head slightly at her words. He was so cute that Stevie almost lost her train of thought.

Gathering her wits, Stevie said, "And don't think that's going to work on me. That. What you're doing with your head, Number One. Or you, Number Five.

Don't think that innocent, adoring little look that you're giving me is going to work."

Number Five quacked happily and ruffled his feathers, watching her with big doting eyes.

"Playtime will be restricted to home base, which in your case is Exhibit A." Stevie pointed to the brooder. "See? Plenty of room. You've got your water dish over there, your food dish right there, nice warm snuggly heat coming off the bulbs. There's absolutely no need to leave the box.

"This is your space. And that"—Stevie indicated the bedroom— "is my space. And contrary to what you may believe, my space is *not* your space. Are we clear on this?"

Stevie was answered with six pairs of eyes gazing at her lovingly. "Is that a yes?" she asked after a moment.

"Quack!" Number One seemed to answer for the group. Either that or he was just hungry.

"Good," said Stevie. "I'm glad we've settled that."

Stevie checked on the two wiggling eggs in the incubator, then grabbed her pillow off the bed and snuggled down next to the brooder. The lack of sleep from the night before was beginning to catch up with her, and watching Seven and Eight wiggle in the incubator was beginning to have a hypnotic effect. Pretty soon, she could barely keep her eyes open.

She blinked sleepily. *It wouldn't hurt to close my eyes for just a few moments*, she thought. Especially since she knew it would still be a few hours before Seven and Eight hatched. Plus that way, she reasoned, she'd be able to stay up later in case any of the other goslings decided to hatch that night. With that thought, Stevie's eyelids closed and she was instantly sound asleep.

Stevie thought she was dreaming. Something was tickling her face. It was soft and feathery and reminded her of when Alex teased her with a buttercup or a feather under her chin while she was sleeping. But these feathers were soft and warm against her cheek. Slowly, Stevie became aware of another sensation, a tickling of feathers against her hand where it rested on her stomach.

Stevie's mind slowly cleared from the foggy haze of sleep. She opened her eyes, disoriented for a moment. Then she saw the brooder and it all came back to her. But as she tried to move, her ear encountered a warm fuzzy mass of gosling fluff sharing the pillow next to her head. She very cautiously raised her head and glanced down her body. Sure enough, all six little goslings had somehow managed to escape the brooder and were now snuggled up next to her. One by her ear, one next to her cheek, one by her hand, and three in her arms.

Stevie laughed. It was the cutest sight she'd ever seen. "Okay, so much for the staying-in-the-box rule."

She sat up, careful not to squash any of her little charges. But the moment Stevie moved, the goslings awoke and began honking at her for disturbing their warm bed. "Sorry, guys, but one of us still has homework to do." She paused. "And, let me remind you, homework from the night before as well. So, everybody up."

As she placed the six quacking little goslings back in their nursery, she realized that she was going to have to make the brooder larger and taller, since the goslings could escape so easily as it was. Plus, she'd read that goslings grew quite quickly and would likely outgrow the box completely in a few weeks. The goslings quacked indignantly at being returned to their box. It seemed that they much preferred Stevie's space to theirs.

"Much as I'd like to stay and chat," Stevie told them, "if I plan to get to bed early tonight, I need to get my homework done." She turned toward her desk. Then, as an afterthought, she added, "And stay put."

Surprisingly enough, the goslings immediately nestled down, their innocent little faces staring up at her, their eyes wide with curiosity.

Stevie moved to her desk, opening her history book as she sneaked a quick peek toward the incubator.

Seven and Eight were wiggling madly now, and Stevie knew it wouldn't be much longer before they hatched. Maybe it would be enough time to get her reading done. She quickly flipped to the correct page to pick up where she'd left off the other night, before any of the eggs had started hatching.

When Stevie looked up from the Napoleonic Wars a short while later, she was quite surprised to find all six goslings shuffling around on her biology book, which was on the floor near her feet. Number One was circling the group like a herder, trying to keep them in order. And Number Three kept trying to escape the herd, only to be rounded up by Number One and shuffled back to the group.

It was clear to Stevie that the goslings wouldn't be contained. It would be much simpler, she decided, to let them wander around her room for the time being. She'd just clean up their little calling cards until she was able to build a bigger box.

"You win," said Stevie. "Just don't make too much of a mess. And Number One, as the oldest member of the group, it's your job to keep everyone together." Number One quacked responsibly, and, Stevie thought, with a new air of authority.

It also occurred to Stevie that she really should

name the little tykes. She looked at Number One. He was bossy—just like an older brother, she mused. He was always trying to make his siblings do what he was doing. And Two always seemed to be getting into trouble. For instance, he'd somehow managed to get his beak stuck under the front cover of the biology book. Number Four (who seemed to come to Two's rescue often) got him unstuck by pushing him slightly to one side and backward. Number Three got turned around easily and was the one that Stevie ended up looking for the most. Even now he was headed away from the group as if striking out on an adventure. But before he made it two feet, Number One brought him under control and returned him to the group.

How was Stevie ever going to come up with suitable names for all of them? The more she thought about it, the odder it seemed to call them anything but Numbers One through Six. She watched the goslings for a moment, then made up her mind.

"You guys are officially dubbed Numbers One through Six," she announced. The goslings quacked in response, which Stevie took to be a type of acceptance.

That settled, Stevie selected a pencil from among the few lying on the floor and began answering her homework questions relating to the Napoleonic Wars. She was only partway through the first question when she was interrupted by a chorus of excited quacks. She looked down to see all six goslings chewing on the rest of the pencils.

"I think I'll take those," said Stevie, quickly gathering up the pencils. Pencils certainly couldn't be good for newborns.

However, as she reached for the last of the pencils, she realized it was attached to Number Six, who had the eraser held firmly in his beak. "Hey, you, let go."

The gosling took a step backward, tugging on the pencil. He seemed quite unprepared to give it up until Number One honked angrily at him. Number Six released the pencil, madly fluffing up his feathers in what Stevie could only describe as a goose fit.

"Thank you, Number One," said Stevie. She placed the pencils on her desk, then thought better of it and moved them to a drawer, closing it firmly. "At the rate you guys are growing, you'll be up here in no time at all." The goslings responded with a harmony of quacks.

Stevie pushed her history book away and checked the incubator. "Well, hello," she said to Numbers Seven and Eight, who had now completed the hatching process and were strutting around the warm incubator in a wobbly, unbalanced way, ruffling their damp feathers as they waited impatiently for Stevie to notice them.

Very gently, Stevie removed the goslings from the incubator and placed them in the brooder beneath the warm lightbulbs. Then she replenished the food and water, which immediately became the main attraction for Numbers Seven and Eight.

"As soon as you two are strong enough," Stevie told them, "you can come out and play with the rest of your brothers and sisters."

Numbers One through Six gathered on Stevie's biology book, watching her attend to the newborns.

Stevie crossed back to her desk, noticing that as she did, the goslings all shuffled slightly to the left to keep her in view, their big dark eyes fixed on her every movement. As she took a seat in the chair, the goslings settled down into a ruffled mass of feathers, their necks craned upward to keep an eye on Stevie.

Stevie glanced at her watch. It was already eight o'clock. She really needed to get her homework done and get to bed or she'd end up just as tired the next day as she'd been that day. With that thought in mind, she pulled her history book toward her and began rereading the first question at the end of the chapter. Once she settled into the work, it only took her another half hour to complete the questions.

Relieved that she'd finally made it through her history homework, Stevie closed the book with a thud. She stood up and stretched, reaching toward the ceiling with her fingertips as she straightened out her back. She figured she'd earned a five-minute break, enough to take a short trip to the bathroom, before moving on to her English homework. All she had to do was make it through two chapters of *Animal Farm* and then she could call it a night.

Stevie walked across the room, pausing at the sudden commotion behind her. She turned to see what the goslings were up to. Numbers Seven and Eight had politely remained in the box, being much too interested in sleeping to care what the rest of their siblings were up to. Numbers Two through Six, however, were at the mercy of Number One, who seemed to be quacking orders at them. Stevie laughed. It reminded her of her and her brothers.

"I think I might nickname you Chad," she said to Number One. Number Three tried to make a run for it, but One quickly intercepted, quacking ferociously. Three meekly returned to the group.

Stevie opened the door and stepped out into the hall. As she turned to close the door, she noticed that the goslings had fallen into single file, with Number One leading the group toward the door. "That's far enough, guys," said Stevie.

The little band of goslings continued their forward march, quacking at Stevie.

Knowing that her mother was unlikely to be amused by gosling droppings in the hallway, Stevie carefully shut the door before the goslings could reach her. There was a moment of silence on the other side, immediately followed by the loud, indignant quacks of six offended goslings.

BY FRIDAY EVENING of the next week, several things had become perfectly clear. The first was that Stevie had become the adoptive parent of eight very healthy and very active goslings, all of whom had decided that she was their mother. They followed her every movement with rapt attention and gazed at her adoringly every chance they got. If Stevie sat at her desk, the goslings sat at her feet. If Stevie crawled into bed, the goslings cuddled up next to her.

The second thing that had become clear was that an entire week had passed without any sign of a wiggle from the four remaining eggs. The accompanying literature said that it was possible that not all of the eggs would hatch. The book also gave instructions on how to candle the eggs to see if they were healthy or not. Although it was a task that Stevie was dreading, she realized it needed to be done.

"Thanks for helping me out with this, guys," she said gratefully.

Lisa and Carole had arrived a short time earlier. The three girls were now in Stevie's bedroom, sitting by the incubator. The eight little goslings were, for once, seated quietly.

"That's what The Saddle Club is for," Lisa replied gently.

Stevie closed the window blinds and shut off the light. Once the room was in total darkness, the girls took one egg at a time and held it in front of a flashlight. The literature provided several different diagrams, explaining what a healthy egg should look like. It also gave examples of what they termed "bad eggs," in which a small dark spot could be seen in the middle of the egg, indicating an expired peep.

After they checked the last egg, Lisa clicked off the flashlight and Stevie turned the bedroom light back on. They'd identified a small dark spot in each of the four eggs, and Stevie knew now there was no hope that the remaining eggs would hatch.

"That's it, then," Stevie murmured, surprised that the thought of the last four eggs not hatching bothered her so much. But, she reasoned, she had watched them and loved them, even though they were just eggs. And now the realization that they would never join their siblings saddened her.

Aware that this would likely be the outcome, Stevie had already gotten her father's permission to bury the eggs in the backyard. Lisa, Carole, and Stevie now made their way out to the backyard with the eggs tucked carefully into a small basket. They were crossing the lawn when a sudden indignant quack from behind halted them in their tracks. The girls turned to see all eight goslings desperately waddling single file and flapping their wings in a not-so-graceful attempt to keep pace with Stevie's walk.

"Oh, look at that," whispered Carole. "They must be mourning their siblings."

Stevie smiled and waited for her feathered family to catch up. One through Seven were moving along quite well. However, Number Eight was slow and kept dawdling. Stevie looped around behind the other goslings, urging him to catch up.

"Come on, Number Eight, move those little legs." Stevie flapped her arms, demonstrating how it was done.

Encouraged, Number Eight made a valiant effort to increase his speed by imitating Stevie, his wings flapping wildly as his little webbed feet scurried along the ground. He only made it a few steps, though, before a weed caught his interest and he began dawdling again.

As if sensing that Stevie and Number Eight needed their support, Numbers One through Seven looped back as well, until there was a small crowd surrounding Number Eight. While Carole and Lisa waited patiently, the little group slowly made its way to the burial site.

Stevie used her father's shovel to dig a small hole, two feet deep into the earth. The goslings, of course, insisted on helping, playing in the loose dirt as Stevie shoveled it to the side of the hole. Then the girls knelt beside the freshly dug grave and watched solemnly as Stevie gently placed the eggs in the ground, one at a time, far enough apart that they wouldn't hit against each other and break.

"Take care, little eggs," whispered Stevie, close to tears, as she carefully replaced the dirt, filling in the hole. She patted it down with her hands, smoothing the soil on top. Suddenly, eight pairs of webbed feet surrounded Stevie's hands, tapping on the earth as they mimicked Stevie's movements.

The girls giggled. It was just like Stevie's goslings to be able to make them laugh when they were sad.

"Hey, they've got better rhythm than you do," Lisa teased Stevie.

Stevie smiled and wiped the perspiration from her brow. "You know, I think a swim would be nice right about now. Anyone up for it?" One of the really good reasons to visit the Lakes during warm weather was the fact that they had a swimming pool.

A chorus of nods and quacks indicated that the idea was a good one. The girls quickly changed into their bathing suits and made their way to the pool, eight little goslings following on their heels.

Stevie walked out onto the diving board, but as she prepared to jump off the end, there was a panicked shout from behind.

"Stevie, wait!" hollered Lisa. "You're not alone up there!"

Sure enough, a procession of eight had followed Stevie up onto the diving board and were prepared (or so it looked from the flapping wings) to follow Stevie off the end into the water.

"I really don't think we should be working on your diving skills just yet, little ones. Back you go."

Stevie herded the goslings off the diving board and walked around the pool to the shallow end. The goslings followed, waddling as fast as their little webbed feet would allow. Stevie took a seat at the edge of the pool, then gently slipped into the water.

"Okay, one at a time, please," began Stevie, adopting her best parental tone. "In a nice orderly fashion—" Before she could even finish her sentence there was a flurry of feathers, followed by all eight goslings jumping excitedly into the water after her, quacking delightedly as they splashed in the pool.

"You guys are worse than Michael!" sputtered Stevie, trying to spit out the large amounts of pool water that she was now swallowing in her attempt to evade the thrilled goslings. But no matter how quickly Stevie swam—backward, forward, or sideways—the goslings were quicker, having instantaneously developed their sea legs.

Lisa and Carole joined the party in the pool, laughing as they played with the goslings. As an experiment, Stevie dived beneath the water, splashing to the surface a few yards away. In an attempt to imitate her, all eight little goslings started dunking their bodies, headfirst, into the water, then popping up for air with a splash.

"What in the world is going on out here?" asked

Mrs. Lake, coming out of the house. "I can hear you girls laughing clear to the front lawn."

"Mrs. Lake, look at the goslings!" Lisa shouted excitedly. "They think Stevie's their mother!"

Sure enough, Stevie was swimming end to end in the pool, accompanied by her eight little friends, who swam merrily beside her, quacking their hearts out.

Enchanted by the sight, Mrs. Lake quickly ran back into the house and appeared a few moments later with a camera.

Mr. Lake, who had also been curious about the noise, joined them as well. He didn't, however, find the sight quite as endearing as Mrs. Lake had, especially as he noticed a couple of small white calling cards floating on the water.

"Stevie—" started Mr. Lake sternly.

"Don't worry. I'll clean them up!" Stevie said before her father could go any further. "I promise."

Alex and Michael appeared from around the side of the house, dressed in their bathing trunks and ready for a swim. They stopped short at the sight of the goslings in the pool.

"Hey, they're swimming!" squealed Michael as he ran to join the girls and goslings in the water.

A moment later everyone except Mr. and Mrs. Lake was swimming around in the pool, playing with the goslings. Alex laughed as Number Three jumped onto his head and flapped its wings. Number Six had become fascinated with Lisa's braids and grabbed on to one, getting tugged about as Lisa swam in circles around Stevie. Carole kept coming to the rescue of Number Eight, who dawdled almost as much in the water as he did on land, and as a result kept getting separated from the group.

After a short while Stevie led the goslings out of the pool, drying each one off carefully with a soft towel to make sure they didn't catch a cold.

Even after Lisa and Carole had left for their own homes, the Lakes were laughing about the swimming goslings. The goslings circled Stevie's chair while she ate, quacking for attention.

"I can't wait to see the pictures you took," Stevie told her mom.

"Let's go swimming again tomorrow," Michael suggested excitedly.

"Um . . . Stevie . . ." Mr. Lake hesitated.

Stevie already knew that look. It meant that her father was going to say something she didn't want to hear.

"We need to be realistic about the goslings," Mr.

Lake began gently. "They're essentially wild creatures, and after a certain point it's not fair to keep them in the house."

"But they're mine," protested Stevie. "Okay, sure, they've been a little messy, but they're babies. And I've been solely responsible for cleaning up after them and taking care of them, just like I said I would."

Mr. Lake stopped eating and gently set down his fork. "Stevie, it's not a matter of responsibility. You've been wonderful with them. But we need to face the fact that they're not exactly house pets."

"But I can train them," Stevie argued determinedly. "I'm sure I can." She glanced at Number One, who was gazing up at her imploringly. She bent down and scooped him up, holding him against her face. "We'll be neater, won't we, Number One?"

Number One quacked in response and gently head butted Stevie's cheek in a show of affection.

"Dad, pleaassseee?" Stevie pleaded.

Mr. Lake had to admit that the goslings were pretty cute. And it was quite obvious from the various looks around the table, including one from Mrs. Lake, that everyone shared the same sentiment.

"All right," Mr. Lake conceded.

"Yes!" squealed Stevie, kissing the top of Number

One's head. The gosling quacked delightedly, watching Stevie lovingly with its large dark eyes.

"But," Mr. Lake said, holding up a hand for quiet, "sooner or later, they're going to have to go. And you should start thinking of a proper home for them."

"*This* is their home," insisted Stevie. "I can't just give them away. They need me." She caught Numbers Two through Eight gazing up at her from their position on the floor beside her chair. "And I need them," she added softly.

After dinner Stevie gathered up her flock and led them back to her bedroom. She placed their dinner in the brooder, watching as they excitedly circled the meal. They greedily filled their beaks with food, dropping more on the floor of the brooder than they actually managed to swallow.

Stevie lowered herself down beside the brooder, staring at them thoughtfully as they ate. Her dad was wrong. There was no reason in the world that goslings couldn't make good house pets. And, thought Stevie, she could provide them with everything they needed to be happy, including their very own swimming pool. Now all she had to do was prove to her parents that the goslings belonged with her, in the house.

STEVIE WOKE UP Saturday morning to find all eight goslings snuggled in bed with her. They grumbled as she sat up and moved them gently out of the way. "Just exactly what are you guys doing out of the brooder?" she scolded them.

As much as Stevie loved having her goslings next to her, she didn't necessarily love the mess they left behind. For instance, they didn't yet understand that the comforter was no place to leave calling cards. Stevie looked around the room, realizing that the comforter wasn't the only place her goslings had been during the night. And as the goslings continued to grow, so did their calling cards.

"Not to mention the food bill," Stevie mumbled, noticing that the bag of chick starter had disappeared quite rapidly that week. She made a mental note to stop off at the pet store on the way home, although she was almost out of money from her last gosling-related shopping spree (materials for the revised brooder).

She thought about asking her father for a raise in her allowance, then shook her head. It was highly unlikely that he would agree, especially since it was to feed her growing herd that he didn't think belonged in the house in the first place. *I'll figure something out*, thought Stevie, *but it's going to have to be later*.

"Come on, guys, breakfast time," Stevie announced, leading the gang back to the brooder. She quickly refilled the food dish, wrinkling her nose at the odor coming from within the box. "Eeeww. Guess this needs cleaning."

Stevie glanced at her alarm clock. Her Horse Wise class started in an hour, which didn't leave her much time to take care of the goslings and get to Pine Hollow. But she couldn't leave the goslings in a dirty brooder all day. Making up her mind, she quickly started cleaning out the brooder, removing the soiled towels and placing them in a garbage bag. She'd find time to wash them later. She reached for her pile of refill towels only to realize that the basket she kept them in was empty. That reminded her that she was supposed to do a load of wash the day before and hadn't gotten around to it.

Stevie hurried down the hall to the bathroom closet and flipped through the towels, searching for one to put at the bottom of the brooder. Unfortunately, the only towels in the closet were her mom's good ones. Running out of time, she grabbed one of those and raced back down the hall to her bedroom, closing the door behind her. *I'll buy another one tomorrow and Mom won't even notice it's missing*, thought Stevie.

Satisfied with her plan, Stevie quickly lined the clean brooder with the towel and replaced the water and food. The goslings immediately hopped into the brooder, slopping breakfast messily in their haste to down the morning meal.

"Guys!" exclaimed Stevie. "I just cleaned that!"

They paused to glance up at her adoringly before quickly returning to the food.

Stevie rolled her eyes. It was no use. She grabbed a washcloth and went about the room cleaning up the mementos left behind by the goslings. It took longer than she expected. She glanced at the clock and hastily pulled on her barn clothes, knowing that the only way she'd be on time now was if she ran all the way.

As it was, Stevie arrived ten minutes late for class. Luckily for her, they were working on their vaulting skills, which meant that she didn't have to groom and tack up Belle, which would have made her even later.

Max gave Stevie a stern look as she slipped into the arena. Tardiness was not a valued quality in his book.

Lisa was up on Clara, working on some of the easier moves at the canter.

"Did I miss anything?" Stevie whispered to Carole, noticing that Lisa had really improved over the past week. She kept her balance in the Stand as Clara cantered in a circle around Red.

"I managed to do the Stand at the canter, too," said Carole.

"Wow!" Stevie was impressed.

"Not very well." Carole grimaced. "But at least I stayed on, which was better than last time. Lisa's doing really well."

Stevie knew that Carole and Lisa had been working very hard on their vaulting skills and deserved to do well in the competition at the end of the month. She felt bad about not putting as much effort into it, but her goslings required around-the-clock care, and she felt even worse about neglecting them.

From the corner of her eye Stevie noticed that

Veronica (in a very un-Veronica-like manner) was standing slightly away from the class, patiently working on various stretches while she waited for her turn.

"What's with that?" Stevie asked Carole, pointing at Veronica.

Carole shrugged. "No idea. The only thing I do know is that she asked Max for warm-up time before taking her turn."

"Warm-up time?" Stevie watched Veronica bend at the side and stretch, her arm curved above her head. She had never seen the other girl warm up in her life. What was even odder was that Veronica seemed in no hurry to take her turn, which was even more out of character than the stretching.

"Maybe she's so terrible she's hoping that Max will forget about her," Carole suggested hopefully.

Before Stevie could think further about it, she heard Max calling her name. "You're up, Stevie!"

Lisa jogged over to them, ecstatic. "Did you see that? I held the Stand at the canter!"

"I'll be lucky if I can hold the Basic Seat," Stevie laughed as she raced off to join Max.

Stevie accepted Max's leg up as Clara walked past, then quickly got into the Basic Seat position. She tried a few moves at the walk before signaling to Red that she was ready to canter. Stevie relaxed, enjoying the smooth feel of Clara's canter. After a moment she swung her legs up and moved into the Flag position. It was the first time she'd tried it at the canter and noticed immediately that she needed to balance herself differently than at the walk.

"Stevie, remember to keep your back straight and your head up," Max offered as Stevie momentarily lost her balance and had to pull her knees back underneath her. "Just get the feel of Clara's stride," he continued.

Stevie closed her eyes for a moment, concentrating on the gentle rise and fall of the canter. It was as natural to her as her own walking. She shifted her knees slightly, relaxing her body. Then she opened her eyes and slowly tried the position again. Releasing one handle, she raised her left hand and right leg, holding the position for one full circle around Red.

"Very good, Stevie," praised Max. He indicated for her to hop down as he turned to Veronica. "Your turn, Veronica."

Stevie slipped gracefully off Clara's back. As she rejoined Carole and Lisa, Max offered Veronica a leg up.

"I think I'd like to try the Flank," Veronica informed Max. "I've been working on it all week with my coach."

Max nodded as the girls shared a surprised look. "The Flank?" mouthed Lisa. Carole and Stevie shrugged.

Gripping the surcingle handles, Veronica confidently swung her legs forward and then back, using the momentum to push herself up into a handstand, keeping her legs straight and firmly together, her toes pointed up. She held the position for two canter strides, then lowered herself gently to Clara's back in a side-seat position.

"Life can't be this unfair," grumbled Stevie. "Tell me I'm just having a bad dream."

"If you are, I'm having the same one," Lisa said, frowning.

"Maybe that's the only thing she's learned," said Carole, trying her best to sound positive.

Unfortunately, it wasn't. The girls watched as Veronica completed the second half of the Flank, in which she once again swung her legs back and up, pushing herself up into a handstand. This time, instead of lowering herself into a side-seat on Clara's back, she used her arms to push herself away from the handles and vaulted backward, landing neatly on the ground behind Clara just to the outside of the longeing circle.

"Excellent, Veronica," Max said as Veronica jogged over to join the other vaulters.

"How could she possibly have learned that in a week?" asked Lisa.

"Let's see. Private coach. Two-hour lessons every day. Hmmm . . ." answered Stevie, now feeling that her accomplishment of performing the Flag at the canter was no longer much of an accomplishment at all. Especially since Veronica's performance had seemed as effortless as if Clara had been standing still.

"She's going to cream us at the competition," said Carole, echoing what Lisa and Stevie were already thinking.

"We're not giving up yet," Stevie said firmly. "There's still time."

With renewed determination, the girls took another turn on Clara. But after Veronica's stunning performance, it was difficult if not impossible to stay positive about the progress they'd made since Clara's arrival. Lisa and Carole did well, but not as well as Veronica.

"So much for that," grumbled Stevie. "There's no way we're going to be able to beat her in the competition."

Lisa was just as bummed out. She released a long sigh, blowing her bangs out of her eyes. "This stinks."

"Guys, we can't let her get to us," said Carole. "Look, I know what will help."

"A private coach?" suggested Stevie.

"No," Carole responded. "A trail ride."

"I don't know . . ." Stevie was thinking that the longer she was away from her goslings, the bigger the mess she'd have to clean up. And then there was all that laundry she had to do.

"Come on, Stevie," Carole encouraged her. "We won't go for too long. And besides, if you don't ride Belle soon, she's going to forget what you look like."

Carole had a point. She'd been so busy with the goslings that she hadn't had much time for Belle. "I guess a short ride wouldn't hurt," Stevie said, grinning.

"And while we're out," added Lisa, "maybe we'll come up with a way to beat Veronica."

The girls nodded in agreement and quickly went to get their horses.

A short while later, Stevie, Lisa, and Carole were galloping their horses across a large open field. They slowed to a walk as they approached a small water hole Max had dug in the middle of the field.

Lisa stroked Prancer's sweaty neck. She was still pumped from the excitement of the run. "That was great!" she exclaimed. "Way to go, girl." Prancer tossed her head and nickered, apparently understanding the praising tone of Lisa's voice.

Carole hopped off Starlight, leading him to the edge

of the water hole for a drink. "Too bad we're not as good at vaulting as we are at galloping," she joked.

But Stevie wasn't really paying attention. Instead she was watching a large crow as it circled the pond. After a moment it swooped down, landed gracefully at the edge of the water, and took a drink. Then it was off again, soaring across the sky.

"That's it!" declared Stevie, startling Lisa and Carole.

"What's it?" asked Carole.

"I don't have to sell my goslings. Or even give them away, for that matter. They can live at Pine Hollow, right here in this field. I don't know why I didn't think of this before!" Stevie exclaimed. "They'll love it!"

Lisa and Carole weren't quite so sure. "What if they don't?" asked Carole. "I mean, right now they're enjoying the comforts of your bedroom."

"Not to mention your swimming pool," added Lisa.

Stevie stared at them for a moment as if they'd each grown two heads. "What's not to love? It's water and they're geese, right? Plus there's all the grass and weeds they can eat. Sure, they're not old enough yet to be on their own, but they will be soon. Until then, I'll just bring them over for visits so that they can get used to their new home."

"Sorry, Stevie," said Lisa, "but this sounds like another one of your harebrained ideas." Carole was wearing a look of agreement.

"Not at all," Stevie assured them. "I'll bring the babies over for class on Tuesday. You'll see. They'll love it here."

"Yes, but will Max love it?" Lisa asked doubtfully. "You know how he gets about your ideas."

"But this time it's a *good* idea," stressed Stevie. Although, truthfully, she thought all her ideas were good ideas. It was just that some of them weren't as well executed or as appreciated as others.

Stevie turned Belle around and urged the mare into a trot. "Come on, I've got to go talk to Max and Mrs. Reg!" Mrs. Reg, Max's mother, was the stable manager.

Lisa and Carole quickly mounted and followed Stevie back down to the barn.

Stevie found Max and Mrs. Reg in the stable office. She explained about the eggs (now goslings) and her dilemma about where to keep them once they got too big to be in the house.

"Well, there's certainly plenty of room here for them," Mrs. Reg said thoughtfully.

Stevie immediately launched into the goslings' finer attributes. "They're really very nice. We've been working on their ground manners and their swimming. And they don't eat much," she rushed on. "Or not too much, anyway. Plus, as an added bonus, they're great for weed control."

Max held up his hands, laughing. "You don't have to convince me, Stevie. I'm fine with the idea. As long as you can convince Numbers One through Eight to stay at Pine Hollow, they're welcome to make this their new home."

Stevie practically ran out the door, forgetting in her excitement to thank Mrs. Reg and Max. She did a quick U-turn and popped her head back in the office door. "Thank you!" she said before darting back down the hall.

CLASS ON TUESDAY was a little strange. Eight quacking goslings were swimming around the horses' water trough while the girls had their regular lesson in the outdoor ring.

Stevie had tried taking the goslings to the water hole. That had started out fine. The goslings had quacked excitedly at the sight of water and immediately dived in, swimming in little circles as they checked out the pond. However, the moment Stevie tried to sneak back to the stable, Number One honked at his siblings and soon had them in an orderly line, following Stevie.

"No, no, no, guys," said Stevie, gently turning them

back around to the pond. "You stay here and I'll be back after my lesson."

The flock of goslings sat at Stevie's feet, gazing up at her expectantly. She dipped her fingers in the pond and played with the water. "See? Water. Bath time for goslings."

The goslings quacked and jumped back into the pond, but as soon as Stevie took a few steps backward, out they came, right on Stevie's toes. Stevie gave a frustrated sigh. She could see that it wasn't going to work. And if she didn't get back to the barn, she was going to be late for her lesson.

"All right," she said, giving in. "Let's go."

The eight little goslings marched behind Stevie to the barn, quacking excitedly at their new surroundings.

Number Eight began to dawdle as usual, so Stevie scooped him up and carried him in her hands. He quacked happily as if that had been his plan all along.

"Freeloader," Stevie scolded gently, not really minding at all.

Back at the barn, Stevie quickly helped the goslings into the trough, then ran to fetch Belle. She groomed and tacked her up outside, where she could keep an eye on the goslings. And as long as Stevie was within their sight, they seemed content to remain in the water trough.

Stevie did fine in her lesson, even when distracted by

the goslings. Max had the class work on basic balancing exercises that would help them with their vaulting skills. Lisa, especially, threw herself into the exercises, hoping it would increase her chance at beating Veronica in the upcoming vaulting competition. And Carole, on her own horse and in her own saddle, did much better with the exercises and didn't even mind when Max had them repeat the exercises over and over.

After the lesson the goslings followed Stevie and Belle into the barn. Stevie was careful to make sure that they walked well out of reach of Belle's hooves. The impatient octet stood outside the stall door (at Stevie's insistence) and waited expectantly while Stevie untacked and groomed Belle.

With a quick good-bye to Lisa and Carole, Stevie made her way outside, goslings in tow, to her mom's waiting car. Since she had thought it'd be too far a walk for the young goslings, she'd asked her mother to drive them over and pick them up.

"How'd it go?" Mrs. Lake asked hopefully as Stevie opened up the rear door of the car and loaded the goslings, one at a time, into a large cardboard box.

"Well, they liked the pond," said Stevie. *For the short time they stayed in it*, she added to herself.

"That's good news, dear." Mrs. Lake smiled at her. "Your father will be relieved to hear it."

Stevie crawled into the backseat beside the goslings and smiled at her mom through the rearview mirror. *They liked the water*, thought Stevie. Now all she had to do was get them to like it when she wasn't around. As Mrs. Lake shifted the car into gear, Stevie protectively dropped her hand inside the box, absentmindedly stroking the little birds' soft feathers.

DETERMINED TO MAKE the goslings adjust to Pine Hollow, Stevie enlisted her mother's help to take them over daily for a quick swim in the pond. Mrs. Lake was more than happy to oblige, especially since Stevie's little charges were growing at an alarming rate and were beginning to get more than slightly underfoot around the house. Stevie had narrowly rescued Number Six from getting flattened when Mrs. Lake went to take a seat on the sofa after dinner, not realizing that Number Six had taken a liking to her favorite spot. And the day before, Number Four had left a calling card in Michael's sneaker, which of course sent Michael into near hysterics when he realized that the warm, gushy feeling he was experiencing as he made his way out the front door was *not* related to the fact that he was wearing brand new gel-padded air treads.

With each visit to the pond, Stevie attempted moving farther and farther away from the goslings while they played contentedly in the water. It was a strategy that had some success, as she was now able to disappear for very short periods of time before the goslings hopped out of the water to come looking for her.

The following Tuesday, Stevie appeared at the barn with her goslings for her regular lesson. Max had scheduled an intermediate lesson for the more advanced students to give the younger students a chance to try some vaulting on Clara.

As had become their daily ritual, Stevie helped the goslings into the water trough. "You guys stay here while I go get Belle."

Stevie needn't have worried. The goslings had become accustomed to the trough and didn't even seem to notice when Stevie ran to get Belle. She quickly tacked up and joined the lesson, which was just beginning in the grass paddock. In the ring next to them, Red was longeing Clara and working on very basic moves, such as riding bareback while holding on to the vaulting handles, with a few of the younger riders.

Stevie took a last quick peek at her goslings, still paddling around the water trough, then got down to work, following Max's instructions as they began the class. They were performing serpentines at the trot and canter without stirrups—an exercise aimed at increasing their balance and suppleness in their lower backs, which would help improve their vaulting abilities.

Midway through the class, Stevie glanced over at the water trough and noticed that the goslings had become distracted and stopped paddling. The focus of their attention seemed to be on Clara and the young vaulters. Despite Number One's best efforts to keep the group organized, Number Three, ignoring the quacks of Number One, climbed out of the trough and waddled over to the outdoor ring. Number Three perched himself just under the fence for a better view of the entertainment. Much to Stevie's surprise, the other goslings followed.

That's got to be a good sign, Stevie thought hopefully. It was the first time she could think of that the goslings had made an attempt to go anywhere on their own that wasn't just to find her. But before the group could enjoy their freedom, Number One rounded them up and herded them back to the trough, honking angrily at Number Three the entire way. Still, thought

Stevie, it was a clear and welcome sign that the goslings were developing some independence.

ON SATURDAY THE girls took part in another vaulting lesson. It was their last scheduled session before the competition, which was to take place the following weekend. Once again, Stevie walked the goslings down to the pond for their daily swim. When she was sure that they were too caught up in their playtime to notice her disappearance, she slipped away and joined the class in the outdoor ring.

"So I wonder where Veronica is," Lisa commented, glancing around as they waited for Max to begin the class.

"I haven't seen her all week," answered Carole.

"Unfortunately, that probably means she's been busy practicing with her private coach," guessed Stevie.

"Let's get started," Max called out, waving his hand for the riders to come forward. "Since this is your last lesson before the competition, I want to see everyone giving it their all."

One by one, the girls took their turn on Clara.

Stevie tried really hard, but the best she could manage was to maintain the Stand on Clara for a couple of canter circles without falling off. She considered it a success of sorts, especially since she hadn't had much time to practice. But it certainly wouldn't be enough to compete against Veronica.

Carole managed to maintain both the Flag and the Mill at the canter, and Lisa was able to do even more than that. She'd finally gotten the feel for the Flank and most of the time was able to execute the first part of it without incident. Unfortunately, Stevie guessed that Veronica had already moved on to more difficult moves that she would use for the competition.

The class was just finishing when Stevie heard the indignant honking of Number One, who, finally noticing Stevie's disappearance, had come out of the pond to look for her. The good news was that it had taken the goslings a lot longer to notice, and instead of panicking, they were now familiar enough with Pine Hollow that they had a pretty good idea of where to find their surrogate mother.

"Hi, guys," Stevie greeted them warmly.

Number One circled behind the group, honking at Number Eight to keep up. One by one, Stevie helped them into the water trough. It was more out of tradition than necessity, since the goslings were now quite able to get into the trough on their own. But oddly enough, instead of paddling around in the water, they all lined up against the edge of the trough to stare at Clara, clearly spellbound by the vaulting horse in the nearby outdoor ring. Red was loosening Clara's surcingle as they finished the lesson.

"I think your goslings have a crush on Clara," observed Carole.

"Either that," laughed Lisa, "or they've never seen anything so huge in their lives."

Red walked Clara out of the ring and brought her over to the trough. Much to Stevie's surprise, the goslings sat quietly while Clara poked her muzzle into the water for a drink. Enraptured, they circled the mare's large face, their beaks tenderly brushing up against Clara's hairy cheek. Clara was unfazed. But then, as the girls had discovered over the past month, Clara was unfazed by almost everything. She simply finished her drink and lifted her head out of the trough, water dripping from her chin. The goslings quacked happily, delighted with the mini-shower that Clara was unintentionally providing.

"Look at that!" exclaimed Stevie. "I think they've found a new friend."

"Maybe with Clara here, they'll want to be here, too," said Lisa.

"It's just too bad that Clara's going home so soon," Carole reminded them.

Stevie realized that Carole was right. The vaulting competition was coming up next Saturday. Right after that, the riders would be saying good-bye to Clara.

It also reminded Stevie that she was running out of time to get her goslings accustomed to Pine Hollow. Her father had hinted again at breakfast that morning that the goslings would soon be too big to be kept indoors. Stevie watched thoughtfully as Red walked Clara toward the barn. The goslings swam to the edge of the trough and honked until Clara's large rump disappeared from sight. Then they returned to Stevie, paddling and honking as they tried to get her attention. Stevie stuck her hand into the trough, splashing them playfully with water. She had to figure out a way to make the goslings realize that they belonged at Pine Hollow—before her dad made some other decision for her.

14

"THIS IS SO exciting. My"—Lisa quickly corrected herself—"*our* first vaulting competition."

It was Saturday morning, the day of the competition, and Carole and Lisa were getting a ride to Pine Hollow with Stevie and her goslings, which were seated patiently in two large cardboard boxes beside Stevie. The goslings had grown so quickly that they no longer fit into one box.

"Did you remember your tights?" Mrs. Lake asked Stevie, glancing in the rearview mirror as she turned up the drive to Pine Hollow.

"Yup, right here." Stevie patted a small bag beside her containing the clothes she'd be wearing for the competition. It was a mix-and-match of gymnastic gear that she'd managed to dig out of her closet.

Mrs. Lake stopped the car in front of the stables and waited while the girls climbed out. Stevie placed the boxes on the ground and tilted them to the side, and the goslings immediately hopped out.

"Thanks, Mom," said Stevie, shoving the empty boxes into the car.

Mrs. Lake leaned toward the open window. "Call me when you're ready."

Stevie nodded.

The girls, followed by the goslings, made their way toward the barn.

"I'll meet you guys inside. I just need to take the goslings over to the pond," said Stevie, noticing that the goslings had already turned down the path in the direction of the pond.

At the pond, they immediately dived into the water. Stevie waited a few moments, then quietly sneaked away. She knew the goslings wouldn't miss her until they became tired of swimming—something that was taking longer each day. She hoped it would take long enough to give her time for the competition.

Back at the barn, Stevie changed into her vaulting outfit and joined Carole and Lisa. Lisa finished braiding her hair and tucked it out of the way so that it wouldn't interfere during the competition.

"Even if we don't win, at least we'll look good," said Lisa.

As much as the girls wanted to do well, they were all aware that their chances against the thoroughly trained Veronica were slim.

"We'll just do our best," said Carole, "which is what matters most in competition anyway."

The other girls agreed. Max was always reminding them that winning was less important than doing your best and reaching your personal goals.

"Besides," added Stevie, "if nothing else, we know a lot more about vaulting now than we did a month ago."

The girls realized that they had learned quite a bit in a month, especially Lisa.

"With any luck, Veronica's grown bored with the whole thing and won't bother showing up," Lisa said optimistically.

"Uh, guys? Don't count on it." Stevie pointed toward the diAngelo's car, which had just pulled up in front of the stables. The door opened and Veronica climbed out of the backseat.

Carole frowned. "What on earth is she wearing?"

Lisa and Stevie were dumbfounded.

"It looks like a . . . costume?" speculated Stevie.

Stevie glanced down at her own mismatched wardrobe, then back to Veronica, who was outfitted in a gold-and-black striped unitard, with gold vaulting slippers on her feet.

"So much for Veronica's losing interest," grumbled Stevie. As usual, the diAngelos had gone to the fashion extreme on Veronica's behalf.

"Not only that, but it looks like she brought her coach," said Lisa.

An older woman, her hair pinned back neatly, also climbed out of the diAngelos' car and was greeted warmly by Mrs. Welch, Clara's owner, who had also just arrived.

As the older women made their way toward the barn, Veronica paused in front of The Saddle Club girls.

"Nice outfits, girls," Veronica commented in her usual condescending tone. "Too bad you couldn't afford something a little more . . ." She paused, searching dramatically for the proper word. ". . . appropriate." She flashed them a smile before heading into the barn.

"Only Veronica would go out and buy a competition wardrobe for something that's not even a competition," Lisa remarked. Then, after a pause, she added, "Why didn't we think of that?"

"Because, fortunately, we don't think like she does,"

said Carole. "Come on, guys, it doesn't matter what she wears or how well she does. What matters is how well *we* do."

"Carole's right," agreed Lisa. "We need to try to forget about Veronica and just concentrate on doing well. In fact, I think it will be fun to be judged by Mrs. Welch."

"Then we'd better hurry and get warmed up or we're going to be late," said Stevie.

While Red longed Clara in a before-class warm-up, Max took everyone through some ground aerobics and stretching exercises. The riders warmed up on the barrel, practicing their vaulting moves, while Mrs. Welch watched.

Mrs. Welch smiled warmly at Stevie as she tried to perform the Flank on the barrel, losing her balance at the last moment and slipping to the mats below. "Next time, Stevie, try to keep your weight centered just behind the surcingle," Mrs. Welch offered kindly.

Although the girls had been thinking of this as a competition, they also realized that it was a great opportunity for Mrs. Welch to give the new vaulters pointers on their technique. Stevie thanked Mrs. Welch for the advice and hopped back on the barrel to give it another try. Sure enough, this time she held the position.

Max smiled. "Very good, Stevie."

Stevie hopped off the barrel, noticing as she did so that Veronica was warming up separately from the group, doing stretches with her coach.

"All right, let's get started." Max waved everyone over to the outdoor ring, where Red was waiting with Clara.

Mrs. Welch, score pad in hand, entered the ring and stood close enough to judge the vaulters accurately but not so close as to interfere with Clara's longeing circle. She nodded to Max to indicate that she was ready to start judging the competition.

Before the warm-up, Max had had everyone pick a number out of a hat to determine in what order they would compete. Veronica and The Saddle Club girls had drawn numbers near the end of the class, with Stevie being the last rider to compete. Stevie only hoped that the goslings wouldn't notice her disappearance before then.

"Since we're pretending that this is a competition," began Mrs. Welch, "I'll ask you to perform as many of the compulsory vaulting positions as you are comfortable with, starting with the Basic Seat. And it's always better to do one move well than to do two poorly." She smiled. "First rider up, please."

The girls watched as each rider took their turn. Max

boosted each rider up, then stepped just far enough out of reach to be of help if he was needed. Finally it was Carole's turn.

"Good luck," Lisa whispered.

"Don't break a leg," Stevie said, grinning.

Carole smiled nervously and signaled to Mrs. Welch that she was ready to begin. Mrs. Welch returned the smile, which Stevie could tell made Carole feel better. Max boosted Carole onto Clara's back, and a moment later she was confidently cantering around the circle, her arms extended in the Basic Seat. Next she performed the Flag, bringing her knees beneath her, then sliding her legs out across Clara's broad back. She held the position for a moment before regaining her balance to move on to the Stand.

Then Carole slipped.

She tried to reach for the handles but wasn't quick enough and fell off to the side. She landed on the ground and ducked into a roll to ease the impact. Stevie and Lisa cheered supportively as Carole jumped to her feet.

"You did great," Lisa said, patting Carole on the shoulder as she joined them.

Carole smiled, pleased with her attempt. Even though it wasn't perfect, it was as good a job as she'd done in practice, and she was pleased with what she'd learned over the past month.

Veronica was up next. She entered the ring carrying a portable CD player, which she placed on the fence near her coach.

"She's got music?" Lisa gasped.

The girls exchanged looks, feeling any hope of beating Veronica draining away by the second. Even Mrs. Welch seemed impressed.

"When you're ready, Veronica," said Mrs. Welch.

Veronica nodded to her coach to start the music, then indicated to Max that she wouldn't need an assisted mount.

The girls exchanged stunned looks. They all knew that an unassisted vault, or a Vault-on, was one of the more complicated moves because it was important not to pull on the surcingle while mounting. Max had explained that it could cause stress or injury to the shoulder muscles on the left side of Clara's body. Max glanced at Veronica's coach, who nodded her approval and smiled.

Veronica slipped into the longeing circle and loped along beside Clara, who was cantering smoothly. Red lifted the longe line slightly to allow Veronica to duck underneath and get into position beside Clara's shoulder.

"Do you really think she can do it?" Carole asked, amazed.

Before either Stevie or Lisa could respond, Veronica reached for the vaulting handles. Using the momentum of Clara's stride, she bounced off the ground, effortlessly pushing herself up onto Clara's tall back.

Overconfident, Veronica started her routine, moving quickly into the Flag. But she slipped bringing her knees underneath her and tumbled off Clara's back, rolling as she hit the ground.

Max offered her a hand up. "That's too bad, Veronica. You had a great start." He was about to call the next vaulter forward when Veronica stepped in front of him.

"But I can't be finished, Max," Veronica whined. "I've got a whole routine worked out."

"I'm sorry, Veronica, but it wouldn't be fair to the others to let you go again."

"But I worked so hard!" Veronica implored. "Please just let me have one more chance."

Max hesitated. "Well, it's not up to me, Veronica," he said finally. "It's up to the other riders."

As Veronica stared expectantly at the group, The Saddle Club girls looked at each other, torn.

Stevie shrugged. "It *would* be a great way to keep Veronica from stealing first place."

"But technically," Carole pointed out, "it's not a real competition."

"And we're all supposed to be here to learn," Lisa agreed reluctantly.

"Even if some of us"—Stevie looked directly at Veronica— "cheated by hiring a private coach?"

Veronica crossed her arms and began to tap one slipper-clad foot with annoyance as she overheard Stevie's last comment. Max glanced around at the group as he waited for their decision. There was a long pause as the vaulters looked at each other.

Then Stevie heard herself saying, "She *has* worked pretty hard over the past month." She abruptly covered her mouth, mumbling between her fingers, "Tell me I didn't just compliment Veronica."

Carole grimaced ruefully. "I think you did. But I agree. Veronica deserves the chance to show everyone what she can do."

"And I have to admit," Lisa added with a smile, "I am just a little bit curious."

"Does anyone object?" Max finally asked the group. Everyone shook their heads. "All right then, Veronica—one more chance."

Veronica smirked and signaled to her coach to

restart the music. Once again, she vaulted smoothly onto Clara's back, and, more cautiously this time, she began her routine. The Saddle Club girls couldn't help being impressed. Veronica performed all the compulsory movements, as well as a couple of freestyle moves that she'd invented with her coach. She ended the demonstration with a proper dismount, landing lightly on her feet.

Lisa groaned. "As if I can beat that!"

"Now that you mention it, we probably shouldn't have given Veronica that second chance," Stevie cracked with a good-humored laugh.

"Just do your best, Lisa," said Carole.

Lisa nodded and jogged over to where Max was waiting. He quickly boosted her up, then stepped back as she began the sequence of vaulting positions. Respectably enough, Lisa managed each one of the four basic positions she'd practiced—the Basic Seat, the Flag, the Mill, and the Stand—before executing a graceful dismount and landing on both feet.

Stevie and Carole cheered wildly for her, as did many of the other students. But they both knew it wouldn't be enough to beat Veronica.

Finally it was Stevie's turn.

Stevie gulped when Red nodded to her. Show jitters weren't something that she was accustomed to. *But then again*, she thought wryly, *neither is performing gymnastics on a moving floor*.

She ducked under the longe line and accepted a boost up from Max as they walked alongside Clara. Taking hold of the surcingle handles, she settled gently onto Clara's back. Stevie stretched her legs downward, comforted by the warmth of Clara's coat against her calves. No matter what she was about to do, it was riding, and riding always calmed her. Well, almost always. As Red clucked Clara into a canter, Stevie instantly relaxed her lower back, allowing her good training and natural ability to take over. Swinging her legs up under her in a crouch, she concentrated on the ripple of movement beneath her knees as Clara's back muscles rapidly contracted and expanded with each rise and fall. She adjusted to the rhythm, and when she was ready, she extended her right leg back and her left arm forward into the Flag. She was surprised by the sudden odd sound around her. It took a second to realize it was applause. She'd done it right!

Smiling to herself, she inhaled the comforting aroma of Clara's musky scent, then began her next move: the Mill (or the around-the-world, as Stevie liked to refer to it) in which she had to turn in a full circle on Clara's back. In the middle of it—just when Stevie thought she had it made—Clara stumbled slightly, causing Stevie to lose her balance and fall against the mare's withers. Clara quickly righted herself, hardly missing a beat, and shifted her own weight to help Stevie recover her balance. As soon as she was comfortably upright, Stevie gently stroked the soft hair at the base of Clara's neck. "Thanks," she whispered. Clara's ears perked up and rotated back in response to the sound of Stevie's soothing voice.

The explosion of clapping from the sidelines caught Stevie's attention, once again surprising her. This time, Stevie smiled to the crowd. Then, with renewed confidence, she brought her legs up to a crouching position as she prepared to move into the Stand. It wasn't as if she thought she was doing a wonderful job, but she knew she was doing the moves as well as she could. She'd learned something and she was pleased that the onlookers thought so, too.

But what she was about to do, the Stand, made the Flag and the Mill look easy.

"Come on, Stevie, you can do it!" Lisa gripped the top rail of the fence as she mentally went through the moves with her friend, feeling every stride of Clara's canter even from a distance.

Stevie shifted her balance slightly in time with the

gentle rise and fall of Clara's canter, mentally following Clara's footsteps as each large hoof hit the ground and feeling her own body and balance become one with the horse. *One-two-three, one-two . . .* She released the vaulting handles and slowly stood up, keeping her arms in front of her as she straightened her legs to a standing position. She felt herself tipping slightly to the right. *No, no,* she thought. She kept counting and closed her eyes, feeling her feet melt into the mare's back, flexing her knees with every stride until she was standing, perfectly balanced, arms out to the side.

There was a buzz in the audience. Of course there was. She was doing something very difficult and she'd done it right. Well, maybe not gold-medal right, but right. So why were they buzzing and not clapping? Keeping her head absolutely still, she let her eyes play across the crowd. They didn't even look like they were about to clap. They looked like they were about to laugh.

Her tights! They must have fallen down! But when she glanced down to check, it wasn't tights she saw at her ankles. It was something fuzzy, web-footed, adoring, and utterly cute. It was a gosling, standing on Clara's back, right behind her! No, there were two goslings! Number Three was there on Clara's rump, and when Stevie glanced down again, Three had been joined by a bossy and irritated Number One, who began quacking authoritatively. He took the position closest to Stevie over Three's quacked objections. They were both silenced when Number Two jumped off the fence to add his performance the next time they circled the ring.

Stevie started giggling. It confused poor Clara, who speeded up. That caused the goslings to quack wildly. Stevie flailed her arms in the air in an attempt to regain her balance. And that caused three goslings to begin flailing their wings in the air in imitation.

And then Stevie heard another sound—one of her favorites. It was the sound of an entire crowd of onlookers laughing with glee.

Stevie knew an opportunity for showmanship when she saw one. Carefully, she settled herself back into a sitting position on Clara's back. She reached behind her with both hands and allowed two of the goslings to settle onto her hands. Then she extended her arms.

"I call this move the Flying Goose," she said, barely containing a smile. The audience applauded. She let Number Three sit on top of her head for a few strides. The audience applauded. Stevie bowed slightly and

Number Three slipped off and then fluttered down to the ground, quacking loudly. Stevie was afraid Clara might unintentionally run over Number Three or—as she realized, when she saw where her little charge had fled—any of the other goslings, all of whom had decided that the schooling ring was much more interesting than the pond that afternoon. Red spotted the problem, too, and drew Clara to a gentle halt. Stevie made as graceful a dismount as she could muster while holding Numbers One and Two in her hands.

The audience burst into applause and Stevie grinned happily, bowing again. The goslings clustered at her feet followed suit, nodding their heads, which made everyone laugh and clap even more. Everyone, that is, except Veronica, who seemed furious to be out of the limelight. She stood behind the rail, arms crossed, tapping one foot angrily, while everyone else circled around Stevie and her adorable little goslings.

"Well," said Mrs. Welch, wiping the tears of laughter from her eyes. "I'm stumped, since it's obvious to me that the blue ribbon really should go to the vaulting goslings."

"But you can't do that," Veronica said hastily. "They're not even part of the competition."

Mrs. Welch nodded. "Which is why I've decided the blue ribbon should go to their trainer, Stevie Lake."

The Saddle Club squealed in delight.

"But—But what about me?" Veronica sputtered angrily above the clapping from the crowd, which also seemed to believe that Stevie and her goslings should be awarded the blue ribbon.

"You did very well, Veronica. Therefore I've decided to award you with the red ribbon."

A warning glance from Max quickly halted the tirade that Veronica appeared to be ready to launch into. "I'm sure that Veronica is quite satisfied with second place," Max said firmly. "Especially considering the fact that she was given two chances."

Veronica smothered a retort and managed a smile for Mrs. Welch. Then she turned to Stevie and whispered, "Cheater!"

But the girls were too busy laughing at Number Seven, who seemed to think that the top of Veronica's slipper would be a good location to leave a calling card.

Veronica frowned and followed their gaze, shrieking as she noticed the white blob left on her slipper as Number Seven waddled away. "You foul beast!" she shouted, then stalked off toward the barn.

"That would be *water*fowl to you," Stevie shouted after Veronica's retreating back.

The girls laughed as the goslings surrounded them,

honking loudly so as not to be forgotten. "Well," said Stevie. "I guess we showed her!"

"Come on," said Carole. "Let's go give Red a hand with Clara."

It was Clara's last day, since the vaulting horse would be returning to her own home the next morning. The girls had planned a special bath and grooming party for the mare to show their appreciation for all her hard work. Not only that, but Lisa had prepared a special apple bran mash for Clara's last dinner at stable.

SEVERAL HOURS LATER the girls shared a late picnic lunch at their favorite spot on the knoll overlooking Pine Hollow. In the grassy paddock below, Stevie could see all eight goslings swimming around in the pond, enjoying the afternoon sun. More noticeably, they seemed not to mind that Stevie had gone off and left them.

"Did you see Veronica's face when Mrs. Welch handed you the blue ribbon?" said Carole. "I thought she was going to explode."

"Well, you know how I hate to gloat . . . ," Stevie answered demurely. She was instantly rewarded with a carrot stick to the side of the head, compliments of Lisa. Her friends knew that Stevie loved to gloat, especially when it came to Veronica. "But," Stevie continued, "what can I say? My goslings seemed to hold better form than Veronica did."

"They did have pretty good balance," teased Lisa. "Perhaps you've found a new hobby for them."

"You know," Stevie said slowly, "there may be one slightly greater victory today than beating Veronica. Although," she added as an afterthought, "that admittedly is a pretty great victory as far as I'm concerned."

Lisa and Carole looked at each other. What could possibly be greater than beating Veronica?

"Earth to Stevie," said Carole. "What are you talking about?"

"Since neither of you two have noticed . . . ," replied Stevie, shaking her head in mock disgust. "It seems that Numbers One through Eight truly are my children, because they've taken on my most desirable quality."

"What's that?" asked Lisa, stumped. Not that Stevie didn't have desirable qualities—she just wasn't sure which one applied to the goslings.

"Well, they seem to have become horse-crazy. Look for yourselves." Stevie pointed to the pond, where the goslings had been joined by Nickel. Three of the goslings were poised on Nickel's back, honking delightedly at the free ride. The others waddled around the pony's feet, trying to figure out how to get on.

Number One, in true leadership fashion, sniffed at his face while he drank from the pond. He honked to get Nickel's attention and was rewarded with a gentle sniff as Nickel investigated his new friends.

The girls watched in amazement as Number One herded up the remaining goslings and steered them toward the water. Nickel, following the goslings' lead, carefully made his way into the pond for a swim. The three goslings on his back slid into the water once it reached their level, joining their siblings and Nickel for a swim around the pond.

"It looks as if your goslings have adopted Nickel," Lisa said softly, smiling at the sight the pony made, swimming around the pond with the goslings.

"I only hope he knows what he's getting into," joked Stevie.

"It seems like everything worked itself out," Carole mused. "You won the competition *and* your goslings have found a new home."

Stevie lay back on the blanket and shut her eyes contentedly. Everything had definitely worked out. "At last," she sighed, "I'll have a good night's sleep and a clean room!"

Lisa and Carole exchanged amused smiles. As if sensing their reaction, Stevie opened one eye. "What?"

"Oh, Stevie," Lisa teased playfully, "you're never going to have a clean room!"

The girls laughed, enjoying the warmth of the afternoon sun while they watched the goslings playing with Nickel in the pond below.

ABOUT THE AUTHOR

BONNIE BRYANT is the author of more than a hundred books about horses, including The Saddle Club series, The Saddle Club Super Editions, the Pony Tails series, and Pine Hollow, which follows the Saddle Club girls into their teens. She has also written novels and movie novelizations under her married name, B. B. Hiller.

Ms. Bryant began writing The Saddle Club in 1986. Although she had done some riding before that, she intensified her studies then and found herself learning right along with her characters Stevie, Carole, and Lisa. She claims that they are all much better riders than she is.

Ms. Bryant was born and raised in New York City. She still lives there, in Greenwich Village, with her two sons.